Other books

Maybe God wa... ...man

Maybe God is an American

If I came back from hell

A sign of signs

*

Dear Daughter

*

Keiko

Copyright © 2020 by Bernie Donnelly

God is an Alien
by Bernie Donnelly

Cover design by AimeeGriffdesigns

Printed in the United States of America.

ISBN: 9781694730435

All rights reserved solely by the author. The author guarantees all contents are original and do not infringe upon the legal rights of any other person or work. No part of this book may be reproduced in any form without the permission of the author.

Disclaimer
This book is a work of fiction. Names, characters, places, and incidents either are the product of the author's imagination or are used fictitiously, and any resemblance to actual person's, living or dead, business establishments, events or locales is entirely coincidental.

For my son, Robert.

God

Is

an

Alien.

"Perhaps my greatest wisdom comes from the knowledge I do not know."

John Steinbeck

Chapter One.

Dr. Noel Clay sat at his desk and wondered was he going mad! He placed his head in his hands and rubbed his fingers hard through his hair in frustration. He closed his eyes tightly and let out a bellow that echoed off the walls. The door to his office opened almost immediately, and a blonde-headed attractive woman peered in from behind the door -

"Is everything all right, darling?" she asked, anxiously. He looked at her for a half-moment as if she was a stranger, before responding -

"Yes, everything's fine, Sam. Just having a moment, that's all." Samantha Clay shook her head and smiled before closing the door, leaving her husband to his thoughts and his outbursts. Having been married for the past twenty years, she knew him and his moods so well and could tell him how he felt before he knew it himself. Sam went back to her own office which was across the hall from his and sat down at her desk, placing her coffee mug on a napkin beside her computer. She had reached a wall in her writing on juvenile cardiovascular practices. It was a difficult subject at the best of times, but trying to explain it to the committee was proving difficult, mainly as her research was not complete. She would have preferred to produce her report in another six to nine months when she could merge her findings with those of her colleagues. She immersed herself in her thoughts, completely forgetting about her husband's earlier verbal emission.

Dr. Clay looked again at his most recent list. He had reduced the names from an original count of over 100 to a single page numbering 18. He re-read the letters he'd sent over six months ago, even though he knew them by heart. The first one read;

My esteemed colleague,

It gives me great pleasure to invite you to a gathering of like-minded individuals this coming July. I know the subject matter will intrigue you. I apologize in advance that I cannot be more specific about the seminar's content. I ask you to put your trust in me on the basis that it will be a unique experience.

I attach the traveling schedule and arrangements, and I would greatly appreciate your R.S.V.P. in the sincere hope that it will be a positive response.

Looking forward to meeting up with you,

I remain,

Yours in earnest,
Dr. Noel Clay,

Dr. Clay didn't have to use any acronyms to describe his many educational qualifications. He was considered the world's foremost theoretical physicist and recognized wherever he went in the world. He was the one responsible for determining the existence of dark matter back in 2009, followed by his contribution to the discovery of the 2015 super-massive black hole. Both of these scientific events added to his already prestigious fame woven over the years by his many television appearances and books that were consistent New York Times favorites. At age fifty-four, he was the shining light of the scientific community and the profession's 'rock star' of the ages.

He read the second letter that he had sent to other notable 'non-science' people, who were as important in their own right for what he was trying to accomplish. It read;

"Dearest friend,

I am inviting you to witness and experience a genuinely ground-breaking event that is due to take place this coming July. I'm afraid I cannot divulge any information as to its content, suffice to say that I would not waste your valuable time. I do hope that you will entrust the weekend in question to attending, even though it is light on detail.

I attach the traveling schedule and arrangements, and I would greatly appreciate your R.S.V.P. in the sincere hope that it will be a positive response.

I look forward to meeting you then,

I remain,

Yours in earnest,

Dr. Noel Clay.

He sipped his now cold coffee as he pondered the list of those who had responded. Of the 18 invited, only three had declined. The three decliners had given good reasons for their non-appearance, which were unavoidable due to illnesses in two cases and a daughter's wedding in another. He looked at the highlighted 15 attendees and hoped he had chosen wisely. He had spent the past year devising the list, and it was as diverse a group of people as he could imagine. The science attendees were easy to select, as he knew all of them and had no difficulty in choosing those most relevant to his agenda. The other notables were selected based on their worldwide prominence and value to the cause. As a scientist, Dr. Clay needed proof and Rapoe had provided all of the evidence necessary for him to make up his mind to go ahead with this weekend's event.

His problems were many, not least of which was attempting to do everything on his own to get the required result. Secrecy was paramount as was the need to give everybody enough time to plan their agendas to have them all arrive on the same day. At the planning stage, it looked doable, but it didn't take very long for him to realize he had set himself an impossible task. He had divorced himself from his day-to-day work and from public circulation to concentrate on the matter at hand. Dr. Clay soon realized that he needed help as he couldn't do the job on his own.

It had taken him some time to get to meet the people that could be trusted to make things work. His most significant difficulty by far was trying to convince people that he was serious about what he was trying to achieve. He had feared that they might treat him with contempt when they heard what he had in mind. Instead, they were professional from the outset and had reacted positively to his proposals and requests. The evening following his first full meeting he received a call that operation *'Clay-Rapoe'* was a go and that someone in command would be in touch.

That, someone, turned out to be a General John Blenfold. *'The General'* - as he was known - was not someone to suffer fools - gladly or otherwise. He had risen to the top tier in the Pentagon through sheer drive and determination. The top brass knew that they needed men of his caliber that could be trusted to bring to fruition those assignments that nobody else could handle.

The *'Clay-Rapoe'* was one such assignment that nobody wanted. The general examined every little detail in his stoic manner. He didn't display any emotion, neither admiration or contempt, as he studied the mission at hand. There was never any question in any of the hierarchy's minds that the general wouldn't take it on. They could go about their business with complete confidence in the success of operation *'Clay-Rapoe.'*

When Dr. Clay first met the general, he didn't know what to expect. The general went into active-duty mode from the outset, treating Dr. Clay like his second in command. The general wasn't interested in the content, which surprised Dr. Clay. Dr. Clay realized he had made the correct decision to get help within ten minutes of meeting the general. It meant that Dr. Clay could relax for the first time since all of this happened. The general assembled a small, but highly trained and sophisticated team of professionals to run the mission. All matters relating to security, confidentiality, and travel arrangements, were under his control. The biggest unknown was how to gauge the attendee's reaction and what to do about their departure should things go awry? Neither Dr. Clay nor the general were able to anticipate that eventuality and could only address the matter if and when it arose.

    Dr. Clay checked the time and decided to take a sleeping pill. He was going to need a good night's sleep before things got underway tomorrow. He checked his itinerary and nodded his approval. Everything would start this coming Friday along the west coast. By then, he would have already set up the welcome for his guests. He wondered, not for the first time, how the world would react when they learned that everything they had believed up to this point in their history was wrong.

Chapter Two.

Lance Wilde sat on his private jet thinking that he hadn't been this excited about a trip since he made his first sci-fi movie over fifteen years ago. He was the complete unknown until the release of the film - *Black Hole* - captivated audiences worldwide, which led to three sequels and the rise to stardom of its lead actor. He couldn't have imagined how popular the franchise had become, nor indeed how his wealth had grown exponentially since those years. Apart from one or two flops, the rest of his movies went on to gross spectacular profits for the producers, garnering three academy awards along the way and the attention of 300 million followers on Instagram and Facebook. His 6ft 4in muscle-bodied frame contributed to his social media numbers. He loved his life and his massive celebrity status. Advertisers clambered to his door whenever they had something they needed to promote, and he was happy to accommodate their needs for a substantial fee. He was wealthy beyond his dreams, and at 45 years of age, he could still command leading roles from all the best studios. His reputation and popularity appeared to be always on the rise, which was why he was thrilled to be asked to attend something by the world-renowned astrophysicist Dr. Noel Clay. He'd met Dr. Clay a few times at various celebrity events, and he was fascinated by the doctor's knowledge of space and the universe. The pilot interrupted his thoughts telling him that they would be landing soon and to secure his seatbelt. A few moments later, his plane touched down at L.A.X. and a private Porsche sports car whisked him away towards the celebrity check-in. He looked out through the darkened windows of the Porsche and was surprised when it sped past the usual check-in door and moved around to the rear of the building. Lance had been here many times as his main home was in L.A. and he wasn't aware of any other check-in area for celebrities. He tried to ask the driver but got no response. The car came to a halt, and the driver jumped out and held the car door open, saying briskly, "Follow me, sir." Lance followed the driver at a quickened pace and was led through two gates, before finally reaching an open area where several people either sat or stood around. Everybody looked his way as the door closed, and a couple of people continued staring, while others went back to what they were doing. He was nearly always recognized, and always felt a little bit peeved when someone didn't seem to know who he was?

"I'll take that, sir," said the driver, already taking Lance's hold-all and whisking it away behind a closed-off area. Lance looked around at the people assembled in the room. There was one woman who was engrossed in some paperwork, while two older men were busily engaged in conversation. A tall, heavy-set, youngish black guy was standing at a window looking out at the aircraft. Lance moved over towards him as he thought he looked vaguely familiar.

"Hi, my name's Lance Wilde."

"Yeh, man. I know who you are. I'm Zapper Zee, but people call me Zapper. Pleased to meet yeh."

"Of course, Zapper Zee - the musician, right?"

"Yeh, Zapper the rapper."

"I knew I recognized you. You're the famous Zapper who's sold more records than the Beatles and Elvis put together," said a smiling Lance.

"And Taylor Swift, and Drake," said Zapper immediately.

"My daughter's a big fan. Here, let me take a photo of the two of us together. She'll love that," said Lance, taking out his cell phone for a selfie.

"I need to take that, sir. No cell phones or electronic equipment allowed until later," said a military-styled man holding his hand aloft. Lance was surprised as he handed over his cell phone.

"They already took mine. I feel naked," added the Zapper.

"And mine too," added a distinguished well-dressed man in his thirties coming over beside them. "My name's Andrew Johnston - with a 't.' I assume Dr. Clay has invited you like the rest of us?" Both men nodded. "I'm well aware of your fame, Mr. Wilde, and I'm sorry to say I'm not a big music fan - of anybody," he added apologetically to Zapper.

"Call me, Lance. What exactly do you do?"

"I'm an astrophysicist at Cornell University. I was intrigued to get Dr. Clay's invitation, but I've no idea what's on the agenda. Do either of you?" Again, both men nodded in the negative.

"What does an astrophysicist do for a living, and who are these other guys that you know?" asked the Zapper, nodding in the direction of the two men deep in discussion.

"I study the universe for a living, and those gentlemen over by that couch are the astronomers, Laurence Shelvey, and Frank Dipple. That person with the beard seated opposite them is none other than Dr. Bill Bardsley of Cambridge University in the U.K. He's the director of the center for cognitive studies and an expert in metaphysics and ontology. The other lady writing is somebody I do not know, but I would suggest she would be another notable in
whatever area of expertise she represents.

"Jeez man. What the hell are we doing here?" asked the Zapper, emphasizing the 'we' to Lance. "I mean all you guys are scientists. Lance and I are just plain old celebrities!

"And rich ones," added a smiling Lance.

"Don't be too overawed by the company," added Andrew. I'm sure Dr. Clay has an excellent reason for inviting both of you. What makes me a little concerned is the whole hidden nature of the thing. I know nothing about the agenda, and I expect it's the same for all of us. I'm also not too happy about the type of security accompanying us," said Andrew, looking around the room, noticing that armed men were strategically blocking all entrances and exits. Lance and the Zapper followed his gaze. They weren't too pushed one way or the other as they were well used to such security intrusions in their lives. The three of them strolled over to a covered table by the wall and availed of the coffee, sodas, and light snacks. A sudden noise made them turn around to see an older man being pushed in his wheelchair by his nurse, obviously annoyed by all that was going on.

"Hand me my briefcase," he barked at the nurse, who bent down and retrieved it from the floor. "Move me over there," he snapped again, pointing towards the lady who had been studying her papers.

"Wow, that's none other than Brian Kingston, the eminent astrophysicist who discovered the planet *Eris* back in 2005, as well as being in charge of the Mars Phoenix lander that confirmed the presence of ice. That's very strange. Kingston would not be a person I would have put on Dr. Clay's invitation list as he is a noted competitor of the said doctor, and I would go so far as to say that they are enemies. What on earth is he doing here? I have to say this little band of brothers is getting more interesting by the minute," said Andrew, drinking some bottled water.

"Ladies and gentlemen, please follow me. We are now ready for the next stage of our journey," said a uniformed military-styled man opening the door to the runway area. Everybody looked at one another and shrugged. They gathered their belongings and followed each other through the entrance to the left of the runway. Brian Kingston was the last to leave the room, accompanied by his nurse. It was a short walk to a hanger door, which, when opened, revealed an air force troop carrier bearing no insignia.

"This way, people, "shouted another uniformed soldier. Everybody was surprised at the outburst and automatically followed one another. They all did as they were instructed and climbed into the available seats. There were no niceties, and no attendants were there to greet them or offer them any refreshments.

"You can sit anywhere you want. Make sure you're strapped in during the journey," said another uniformed man who looked like he was the pilot. An officer assisted the nurse in securing Brian Kingston's wheelchair.

"Where are you taking us?" asked astronomer, Frank Dipple, but he got no answer. Almost immediately, the engines fired up. Lance sat in beside the Zapper, and they were both joined by Andrew. Ten minutes later they were headed out to sea and could barely hear one another over the noise of the engines.

*   *   *   *

John Mahoney looked anxiously around him at the departing gates at Rome airport. He knew he'd have little difficulty in recognizing his companion passenger for today's flight, but he was beginning to show concern that his companion had still not arrived as John checked the notice board which told him that he still had about a half-hour before they'd start boarding. He thought how the past six months had been a bit of a nightmare after he had received Dr. Clay's invitation to a special conference somewhere on the west coast of America. John was heavily involved trying to sort out the problems of the Catholic Church, between the legal actions being taken worldwide against the church's priests for one crime after another; to the massive drop-off in attendances that had snowballed into a global problem. He was forced to ask the Pope for permission to attend this conference as he felt the church needed to keep abreast of everything that could affect their understanding and their teachings. He had been approved to participate once he had explained that the young people today had a highly educated opinion of our planet and our universe and that the church needed to keep informed of the very latest developments. If the eminent Dr. Clay granted us an invitation, then it was for an excellent reason, and it was beholding on somebody in authority to accept that invitation. He had to lie to the Pope when asked about the content of the seminar, and he said that all the world's best theologians, philosophers, and scientists, would be in attendance. John stood up and looked around anxiously for his friend. He noticed that they had made the first announcement for passengers to board.

"Ah, Dan Rosenberg - at last!" he said aloud, relieved that his friend was on his way. A thin elderly looking gentleman was making his way up the center walkway looking from right to left at the various boards indicating that gate's arrival or departure. He looked ahead and saw John waving at him. He acknowledged him and saw that he was gestured to hurry. They shook hands and greeted one another like long lost friends as they lined up to board their flight. As they sat down and made themselves comfortable, John said -

"I see you're not wearing your kippah. Why is that?"

"Nowadays, it pays to be careful about advertising your views and beliefs. I think it prudent not to advertise at all," smiled Dan. John and Dan went way back, having bumped into one another on many occasions and shared many great evenings discussing philosophy over an expensive bottle of burgundy - sometimes two. He was thrilled when he found out that Dan had also received an invitation, as they could both share whatever was about to be revealed.

"I understand the Muslim leader Khalid will also be in attendance," said Dan. John raised his eyebrows quizzically, saying -

"That's news. I would have thought he would be the last person to be invited. When did you find that out?"

"I have my sources. So whatever, or whoever is attending, there seems to be a strong mix of scientists, philosophers, and religious leaders."

"Anybody from the Hindu faith?"

"Not that I've heard. Have you been able to find out who or what we're discussing?" John took a sip of water before answering,

"Not a word, and it's not for want of trying. Of course, I had to keep things a secret as best I could. I know that Dr. Clay asked us all specifically to be discreet. Anyway, Dan, it's great to get together again. Whatever we are about to see, I'm sure we won't be wasting our time, and besides, it's always good to share our views with as many people as possible." Dan thought about his friend's words and remained quiet. He didn't like going into the unknown, and whatever the Americans wanted to speak about, he would continue to stay guarded. "It's a long flight, Dan. First stop New York, then to Los Angeles, so we'd better get some rest." Both men extended their seats to the maximum position and pushed their pillows behind their heads. Dan was asleep almost immediately.

* * * *

Billionaire philanthropist, Edgar Snipes, was not someone who ever did anything without knowing all of the details. When the renowned Dr. Noel Clay sent him the invitation, he knew he could not refuse. Even his wife begged him to include her in the secret rendezvous, but he told her he considered himself lucky to be included on the list. His mind was further salivated by curiosity, knowing some of the greatest scientific minds were also making the same journey? Edgar bid his goodbyes to his wife and was presently awaiting the departure of his private jet to a place unknown. He wondered why his regular pilot and his staff were not around to greet him and look after his needs, and he anxiously checked his watch for the umpteenth time that morning. At last, he saw a vehicle approaching and two men jumping out at the end of the stairway. They were both dressed in a military uniform which unnerved Edgar.

"Better buckle up, sir. We'll be taking off immediately," said one of the men as he sealed off the door. Edgar was slightly taken aback at the rudeness of the man but kept his thoughts to himself when he noticed that the co-pilot was fully armed. The jet took off more suddenly than Edgar was quite used to, and within minutes they were headed west with the sun to his left. Without any means of communication available to him, Edgar had no clue where he was going or how long he would be in the air. When Edgar made tentative and courteous inquiries, he was told in no uncertain manner to prepare for a long flight and to try to get some rest. Edgar then realized that this was going to be a trip, unlike any other he had ever experienced.

Chapter Three.

The pilot of the unmarked military plane announced that they were shortly coming in for a landing and that everybody was to belt up as the runway was short and that the landing could be tricky. It was not the sort of announcement that its passengers appreciated. Lance looked across Zapper's shoulder and saw the blue ocean below, saying -

"I wonder where the hell we are? How long have we been traveling?"

"Over three and a half hours," added Andrew, checking his watch. "And I'd say we're about 1000-1500 miles from shore, due West. It looks like we're heading in the direction of that small island over there," The plane shook slightly, then took a steep turn and dropped down suddenly, giving its passengers no time to get concerned. Within a minute they had landed on the runway. The doors opened quickly, and an officer escorted them to a waiting mini-bus. Only a few soldiers patrolled the ground, and there were no civilians in sight. They drove a short distance to a large metal building that looked like an army barracks. They were escorted inside the building to be met by a smiling Dr. Clay.

"Welcome everybody. Thank you for making the long journey. I hope you were not too inconvenienced, and I promise you that your trip will be more than rewarding." He then shook each person's hand and said, "We are waiting for one other person to arrive, so in the meantime, let's go and meet the rest of the guests." Dr. Clay led the small group to a door that opened into a much larger area, saying, "Okay, everybody. I'm sure you can all introduce yourselves, and I know a number of you are already well acquainted. There are some refreshments scattered around the room." Dr. Clay looked around at his guests, and it began to dawn on him that everything was real and not just names on a sheet of paper. *'No turning back now,"* he thought. He clapped his hands, saying - "Your bags are on their way. I'm afraid the accommodation will not be up to your normal standard, but remember, this is an army barracks used for special operations. I'll explain everything in greater detail as soon as my final guest arrives, which hopefully won't be too much longer. You'll each find a bunk-bed through that curtained off area over there," he continued, pointing towards the end of the room. "There are, of course, closed-off areas for both men and women with separate bathrooms. I hope you will bear with me until I make my full announcements to the complete gathering. Thank you," he said, moving off to the exit accompanied by a stern-looking military man who appeared to be in charge.

"Not the Ritz," said a friendly-looking man to the small group that included Zapper, Lance, and Andrew.

"Hi, I'm Fred Pinkton, NASA physicist," was all he said, as he shook each person's hands. Fred had the dorky looks one would typically associate with a NASA scientist.

"And I'm Dr. Lila Thompson," said a ruffled looking elderly woman muscling her way into the group. "I must apologize for appearing rude during our journey here, but I had to finish a paper I've been working on for some time. I hope you can forgive me?" she asked.

"Not a bit, Lila," added Lance, putting her at ease. "It's my pleasure to know you and Fred. This here is the great Zapper, and this is Andrew Johnston - with a 't'" - said Lance, completing the introductions while Lance and Andrew smiled at his wit.

"What is your field of expertise, Lila?" asked Lance.

"I'm a theological philosopher at Cornell, and I've no idea why I'm supposedly at some science convention?" she said brusquely.

"It appears we all have one thing in common," said Andrew. "We appear to be all in the dark about what is about to occur." They all nodded compliantly.

"I have to say I'm intrigued, and I know Dr. Clay wouldn't waste any of our time unless he thought it was of the utmost importance," said Fred.

"I'd still like to know what the hell I'm doing here," added Zapper, emphasizing himself. "I'm certainly no scientist, and I flunked out of school when I was eleven." There was a silence as the rest of the party wondered what to say. They, too, had wondered about the same thing.

"Not to worry, Zapper. It's you and me both, buddy," said Lance, which deadened the awkwardness.

"We might as well go with the flow until we hear from Dr. Clay, I suppose," added Fred, making his way over to one of the refreshment tables. The rest of the small group followed.

*   *   *   *

The plane carrying Edgar landed smoothly on the small runway. Edgar had tried to pinpoint their position, but he found it impossible without any technology being available to him. All he could discern was they had headed due West for approximately 1000+ miles, more than likely 1400. The pilot announced that they were due to land and to fasten his seatbelt. "The mystery deepens," he whispered to himself, getting more excited now that they were about to land. "Let the show commence," he said as the plane landed smoothly. As he alighted, he noticed a large building in the distance, but nothing else. Edgar was jolted from his thoughts by the sight of a jeep-type vehicle arriving at speed. The driver took Edgar's hold-all and guided him into the passenger seat. The uniformed officer then drove at speed without saying anything until they reached the building that had all the appearance of a military hanger.

"This way please," he insisted, as he led him inside. Dr. Clay greeted Edgar warmly, saying -

"Delighted you could make the journey Edgar. I know you will not be disappointed. Follow me inside to meet the others." As soon as Dr. Clay opened the door, he announced loudly, "Ladies and gentlemen, I am more than happy to present Edgar Snipes." Everybody was surprised to see Edgar Snipes in their presence. The world-famous philanthropist and one of the original fathers of the technology era certainly brought a whole new credible dimension to the proceedings. People immediately flocked towards him, but Dr. Clay raised his hands saying,

"Please, for the moment I'd like everybody to grab a few hours sleep. I'm sure many of you are very tired, and I can assure you that your beds are comfortable, if nothing else. You'll have ample time to get to know one another, and I also know that the conversations will be vibrant. Please follow me and I must ask you to be quiet as there a couple of gentlemen already asleep." He led the way to a cordoned-off area and pulled back the curtain revealing John Mahoney and Dan Rosenberg in deep slumbers. "They had an exhausting trip half-way across the world," whispered Dr. Clay as he tiptoed his way past their two bunk beds and directed people to vacant ones, which stretched the length of the building. A female officer escorted Lila Thompson and the nurse to the other side of the hall.

"We will wake you at 1100 hours. The wash and shower rooms are through either of those doors," said Dr. Clay pointing in two directions. Now I'll leave you all to get settled in. You should re-set your watches to 8 pm local time. I expect to get proceedings underway with a full presentation around midnight. So, please take this opportunity to avail of some rest. Thank you, all," he concluded.

"I don't know if I'm going to be able to sleep. What about you?" asked Lance of Zapper.

"Nah, me neither. I'm a night owl anyhow."

"Mr. Wilde, I wonder could I trouble you for your autograph. I've always been a big fan, and it's not for my daughter, it's for me," said a smiling Lila, handing Lance a pen and paper. Lance was surprised and delighted that Lila was coming out of her shell.

"My pleasure, Lila," taking the paper and scribbling a note followed by his usual handwriting.

"I've loved most of your movies, especially the sci-fi ones from your early career," she said enthusiastically. Lance nodded saying,

"They were my favorites too. I'm making a new one down in Mexico called, *"The Immigrant."* It's an indie movie with myself and Tom Hanks. I'll make sure you get an invite to the premiere." Lila smiled broadly saying,

"Why thank you so much, Mr. Wilde. I'll look forward to it very much."

"And please, call me Lance." Lila continued to look at the inscription which read "To my friend Lila, bright and beautiful." She blushed as she returned to her bunk-bed area.

"Guess it's time to start reading this book I've been carrying around for the past few years. Maybe I'll get some shut-eye," said Zapper, as he lay on his bed. The hall lights dimmed and a steady calm settled over the group.

Edgar waited an hour before venturing to catch Dr. Clay. He walked quietly towards the exit and was shocked to find an armed guard on the other side.

"I'm sorry, sir, but I'll have to ask you to stay by your bed as my orders are to let nobody roam around," he said matter-of-factly, as he drew back the curtain. Edgar was flummoxed. He shrugged and whispered, "Guess that puts paid to that idea." He made his way back to his bed and lay on top. Within fifteen minutes, he was fast asleep.

* * * *

Most of the people had fallen asleep and didn't take too kindly to the rude awakening a few hours later. Eventually, everybody got on with their ablutions quietly, with few words exchanged. The nurse waited to attend to her employer, Brian Kingston. As soon as the last person had exited the shower area, she then wheeled him alongside one of the basins and helped him to freshen up. All the people assembled as instructed having taken what refreshments were made available.

"This coffee's not the worst, but I've had a lot better," said Andrew Johnston.

"You always seem to be in a good mood," noted Zapper. "What's your secret?"

"Not worrying about anything until the problem occurs. That, and having a partner that loves me and whom I adore," he confirmed, which still left Zapper and the others within ear range curious as to whether his partner was either male or female?

"Ladies and gentlemen, if you would follow me outside, you'll find seating arranged facing a small podium. The weather is warm and mild, but not humid. You can take whatever you need by way of refreshment with you to your seat," announced Dr. Clay. Everybody was anxious not to be the one responsible for any delay, so they all collected whatever they needed and made their way past the officers to the two rows of chairs about a hundred yards away from the main building. Dr. Kingston was the last to show, accompanied by his nurse. Finally, all were in position, and everybody wondered about the strict looking man who was never far from Dr. Clay and who now appeared on the small podium wearing a full uniform with an array of stars across his chest. It was evident to everyone that he was someone with authority. Dr. Clay cleared his throat and looked straight ahead at nobody in particular, saying - "Good evening, everybody, or rather a good morning as it's now a little after midnight," he said, checking his watch. "It gives me enormous pleasure that all of you have shown up today, particularly as all of you have been kept in the dark ever since I issued the invitations." Dr. Clay paused as he considered his notes, thinking that everything he had prepared to say seemed trite when compared to the magnitude of the occasion. He looked again at his audience, who all seemed to be hanging on his every word. "Allow me to introduce General John Blenfold," he said, turning around and indicating the man seated to his right. General Blenfold is a 5-star general in charge of the strategic command, which is a covert operations group that encompasses only the most highly trained and gifted personnel. You will see a number of these officers throughout the campus." The general moved his head slightly to one side by way of acknowledgment.

"Don't think I'd go messin' about with the likes of him," whispered Zapper to Lance, who nodded his agreement as he examined the muscular shape of the wise-looking general.

"The general's presence emphasizes the importance of our gathering," continued Dr. Clay. "You are the elite of the world's science community spread across all faculties of the known sciences and are responsible for several findings that have, and will continue to have, a bearing on humanity's future. Also, amongst you, are the world's finest theologians and leaders of various religious communities. We are also happy to have several famous faces joining us whom you no doubt recognize. I asked all of you to maintain secrecy about this weekend, and I'm more than pleased that this has occurred. You will shortly understand why we had to demand such secrecy and, just one moment please," said Dr. Clay as he held his fingers to his temples. He appeared to be in some discomfort, but everybody looked from him to the general seated behind him and noticed that the general showed no concerns whatsoever, which made people relax. It took another minute for Dr. Clay to regain his composure. He turned to the general and nodded, which appeared to be a signal between them. Then Dr. Clay turned back towards the group, saying, "I apologize for that brief interruption, but I'm happy to say that everything will get underway very shortly," he said. There was a little breeze, and the temperature was balmy but not excessively humid.

"Let me explain the geography. We are on an island far out in the Pacific Ocean. It is a secret location known only by the military. It is not on any map and never has been. It is a US territory and used for scientific and military research purposes. It is approximately 4 miles long and a half-mile wide. There is only one other small building on the south of the island that houses a small solar generator that provides electricity. There are no civilians stationed here. We needed somewhere unique like this for two reasons. Firstly, the weather conditions were perfect and paramount for our needs. Secondly, it is secluded and away from all prying eyes, which includes navy, aircraft, and satellite infiltration. At this juncture, I will ask General Blenfold to say a few words." Dr. Clay moved to one side while the general stood. His imposing figure ensured that he had his audience's attention as he said -

"The United States Government considers what you are about to witness with the utmost seriousness. I am here for several reasons that include everybody's security and well-being. Nobody inside or outside the government has had anything to do with this forthcoming event. We are not responsible in any way," he concluded rather abruptly and sat back down. Dr. Clay moved forward,

"Thank you, general." Dr. Clay turned his attention back to his audience saying - "I ask each one of you to remain calm and composed at all times. You will have ample opportunity to ask questions and discuss everything that comes before you. Remember, you are here for the weekend. Nobody is in any hurry to leave. Finally, I ask you to open your hearts, and your minds like you've never done before." Dr. Clay stopped speaking and scanned the audience. He could see the excitement was palpable and a number were fidgeting, begging the proceedings to commence. He turned towards the general, who nodded. Then Dr. Clay pointed to the night sky, saying -

"We are ready. I want you all to look out to the East. Presently you will see a bright light which will move towards us very quickly. Don't be alarmed at anything." Dr. Clay turned towards the East as did everybody in the audience. The only ones who didn't look in that direction were the uniformed officers. The silence endured for some minutes until somebody said -

"Look! Over there," said one person, pointing. Some people stood up, which made most people also stand. The light in the distance was thin and traveling at speed. People wondered what type of aircraft it was, as everybody squinted to clear their view.

"It's a meteorite of some description," said astronomer, Frank Dipple.

"No, it can't be. There's no tail," added the other astronomer, Laurence Shelvey.

Within a few seconds, the light was in front of them, which happened too quickly for people to be shocked. It was a soft light that people didn't have to shield their eyes. The light had a movable vapor that had no definitive shape. The object was around 20 feet wide and barely more than a yard in depth. It was suspended about 100ft away and 30ft from the ground. It didn't appear to be an aircraft or have any recognizable design.

"It's amazing! What is it?" asked NASA physicist, Fred Pinkton. "It doesn't have any solidity - it's like a lighted vapor," he said to nobody in particular.

Everybody wondered what was to happen and looked from Dr. Clay back to the light. Dr. Clay didn't move but continued to stand in the same position as if he knew what to expect. There was a muffled sound from the light as if it was about to say something. Everybody was now standing, waiting. Their breathing got deeper as their hearts beat faster. Then they heard their voices emanating from inside their heads saying;

"My name is Rapoe - you know me as God!

Chapter Four.

A cacophony of voices erupted, all directed towards Dr. Clay, who remained stoic and unmoved. He allowed the noise to continue unabated, as General Blenfold stood alongside him. The only member of the audience to stay seated was Edgar Snipes, who found the whole event mesmerizing.

"Is this a joke?" asked NASA physicist, Fred Pinkton.

"Who's idea was it to bring us out here for some reverie…some pie in the sky special effects show," shouted Brian Kingston.

"I won't stay here to listen to heresy and blasphemy, Dr. Clay. Explain yourself," shouted an angry Dan Rosenberg, now fully recovered from his jet lag.

Other comments flowed, laced with annoyance and anger in some cases. It took some time before the tide of abuse quietened to some mutterings, mainly due to theologian, Peter Shapley, who stood up and faced everybody by appealing for quiet to allow Dr. Clay to answer. Most people took to their seats, while the others remained standing. No sounds came from the light known as Rapoe. Dr. Clay had imagined himself in their position had he had no advanced warning. He had estimated that he too would have been annoyed and possibly angry. He waited another moment before saying,

"Thank you, Peter, for your intervention. Let me say at the outset that I expected this reaction. The general and his team had discussed it with me many times. We are not surprised. There was no other way to present this to you. We have no control over this situation, apart from knowing when Rapoe was due to appear." The general stood up beside Dr. Clay and said, "I can assure you, ladies and gentlemen, that what you are seeing has nothing to do with any sector of the American defense forces. The vehicle in question is not a spaceship or a ship of any kind. It has no metal, nor is it made from any known substance. It is a vapor of some sort. We have tried to analyze its structure without success. I will explain this further, later on. Thank you for your patience, remain calm, and listen to Dr. Clay," he said, moving back to his seat.

Dr. Clay then continued - "Let me give you some history up to this moment." The rest of the audience sat and listened attentively. Dr. Clay glanced at the general, who shook his head slightly, affirming it was the correct way to approach it. "About two years ago, my wife and I managed to get away for a weekend break. It wasn't easy for either of us to arrange, but for personal reasons, we knew it was something we had to do. We booked a secluded cabin near the Appalachian trail and found the seclusion we needed. I had been experiencing quite a lot of headaches leading up to our short vacation, and we both felt that we needed some time away together. However, on the second evening, I experienced a type of communication. It's the only way I have to describe it. It was an intense feeling like something I'd never felt before. It was the sound of my voice within me - speaking to me from afar, yet within me. It's a bizarre feeling and one you are about to experience. I couldn't understand it! I could hear myself, yet there was no external sound. My wife, who was sitting next to me reading, didn't hear anything when I asked her. Rather than worry her, I decided to step outside into the night air, hoping that these noises would disappear, only they became clearer. It was 'Rapoe" - the voice you've just heard. He calmed me and assured me that I was in no danger. It was the first of many such encounters. I thought I was going mad. As time elapsed, and the days became months, I had become accustomed to our relationship. Yes, we had built up a relationship. Rapoe didn't appear as you see him now. It was always a voice - my voice - within me, that was the method of communication. When he explained his reasons for choosing me and what he wanted me to achieve, I became naturally intrigued. I became comfortable in his presence, and no longer felt the need for any psychiatric help. What you are about to experience is very real. It's frightening, and certainly illuminating at the same time. You are all here for a reason. Rapoe will explain everything to you, providing - as I said at the outset - that you open your minds and your hearts. It is only by doing this that you will begin to understand what I already know. However, it is beholding upon me to allow Rapoe to speak before I say anything further." He turned to the light saying, "Rapoe." There was a further pause before people heard -

"I will speak to you in your native language and your voice so that you will hear me as others hear you." People looked at one another in shock and distrust, wary of what was to come. They checked their ears with their hands, thinking that they had on headphones. They looked around them and saw nothing, only others doing the same thing. They were outside, exposed to the night. There was no sign of any technology. They all turned their attention to the light. "As Dr. Clay has said, I first made contact some years back. I chose him because of his diverse and scientific knowledge, together with his singular celebrity and status in your world. He has your respect; therefore, he also has mine." Most people held their hands to their ears as Rapoe spoke. They couldn't believe they could hear their voices. Everything was crystal clear. There was no Interference, and it didn't sound like a machine, or a computer was doing it. It was as if they were in a room with only themselves! Others could hear in their language and included the Muslim leader, Khalid, who remained quiet as he listened to the interpretation which he found to be faultless. Most people shook their heads from side to side with amazement and continued to look towards Dr. Clay instead of at the light. However, a certain calm came over them as their heightened curiosity extinguished any further criticism. Dr. Clay noticed the change of mood, and he looked towards the light, saying -

"Please, Rapoe. Continue." Everybody looked again towards the light and heard the following -

"When I first spoke to your prophets Moses, Abraham, and Isaiah, I encouraged them to have faith in me, and that I assured them of their safety. They were great men in difficult and primitive times. If I had appeared to them, the way I am appearing to you at this time, they would surely have not understood and would have been very frightened. To that end, I allowed myself to blend into their ways - to be as one with them so that they could understand and, thankfully, they readily accepted me and believed in me. It was their belief that gave me hope. Maybe it was easier in those days to make men believe, unlike today. In those days, they needed to see signs of my power. I can understand that.

To that end, I created the flood and parted the Red Sea, and more importantly, I gave my commandments. The commandments cannot be understated. I issued them at a time when man had no respect for his fellow man. To follow me, and gain eternal life, humanity had to obey my wishes. It didn't turn out to be that simple. Moses did what he could and suffered because of it. I never forgot him for that. His soul is with me." The ecclesiastics in the audience shuffled uncomfortably, not knowing what to make of this 'Rapoe' and what he was saying. John Mahoney chewed his lower lip, mesmerized by what he heard. Dan Rosenberg remained stoic and distrusted everything he had heard and seen so far. Rapoe continued - "The world's population was not as big back then, as it is now. Everything centered around Jerusalem and Rome. Despite the work of Moses, Joshua, David, and many, many, more, it became a futile exercise, which resulted in the 'silent years' - a period where I removed myself from the happenings of humanity. I knew we would need something else - something far better than what we had attempted to do. I also knew that everything would change, as it always does, and sometimes it is better to do nothing, which is what happened. I couldn't force my needs upon the people for reasons which will shortly become clear."

A few people were decidedly perplexed listening to Rapoe, as the content was not something they wanted to hear. They muttered amongst themselves. Rapoe remained silent while this was going on. Dr. Clay looked down at his audience and smiled quietly. It was what he had hoped would occur.

"May I speak to Rapoe, Dr. Clay?" asked Dr. Bill Bardsley. Dr. Clay nodded in the affirmative. Bill Bardsley turned to the light asking,

"Why don't you show yourself? Perhaps, if we saw you in the flesh, then we could take you more seriously." Most people nodded and began to go silent, waiting on Rapoe to respond. They didn't have long to wait.

"I cannot appear as you requested of me. I don't have a physicality." Upon hearing this, most people gasped audibly. Rapoe continued, saying, "I should explain further so that you can understand more. I have never controlled you, as some would like to believe. I always stood apart, unless I felt I needed to help, as in the case of Moses and Noah. There is a straightforward explanation for this." People hung on to his every word and wondered what Rapoe was about to say. Dr. Clay held his hand aloft beckoning people to sit down and remain calm. Another five minutes elapsed before Rapoe said - "I did not create the earth - I found it!"

Immediately, everybody jumped to their feet when they heard this, and turned to those around them, expressing their shock and disbelief. There was a crescendo of noise as people spoke to one another trying to make sense of what they had just heard. The science fraternity was enthralled, and seemed delighted with Rapoe's statement, while the philosophical community was intrigued and wondered what other revelations would unfold. The religious community was in an uproar. Dr. Clay stood beside the general and looked down from the podium wondering if Rapoe was going to deliver another body blow? Then Rapoe continued, saying -

"As Dr. Clay said at the outset, you need to open your minds, and your hearts for I have a lot of truths to unfold before you. As I said, I did not create your earth, I found it, as I have found many other planets. There is something fundamental that you should also know. It is the very essence of my visit, and something you will have to understand." The audience remained very still. They were in a daze, their minds swirling in confusion at what they'd just heard, only to be shocked to their core when they heard him say -

    "I did not create you - I found you!"

Chapter Five.

There were gasps all around, then the light disappeared. Everybody stood, except for Dr. Brian Kingston, who was demanding that his nurse wheel him to the stage.

"This is ridiculous. I need to speak to Dr. Clay," he insisted, as the nurse tried to guide his wheelchair through the crowds who were also clamoring for Dr. Clay.

"What's going on? What's happening?" said one voice after another.

"Perhaps we should take some time out to discuss what we've heard," shouted Dr. Clay above the noise. "I will be available to every one of you, but not at this moment. Please discuss what you've seen and heard between yourselves. Rapoe is not gone away. He advises me that we all need to consider his words. He will return when I signal him. Thank you, ladies and gentlemen." The general announced that people should move back inside for some refreshments and to use the bathroom facilities.

"Holy crap. I never expected anything like this," said a gob-smacked Lance to Zapper, who was shocked like everybody else. He looked up at Lance, saying -

"You, me, and everybody here, my brother. Talk about surreal! I think I have enough material here for about fifty albums."

"Extraordinary," countered Andrew Johnston. "I can't believe what we've witnessed. Extraordinary," he repeated.

"What did you make of it all?" asked John Mahoney of Dan Rosenberg who continued to stare straight ahead. John waited until Dan said,

"This goes against every teaching in the Old Testament and, I believe, everything that you have ever learned. It's not just heresy; it's blasphemy of the highest order. I'm not staying to listen to anymore. I'm leaving." John was shocked at Dan's reaction.

"But, Dan, there's a lot more to happen. A lot to be said. I'm certain of it. You must stay," he pleaded.

"Nonsense. What we've witnessed is beyond a joke."

"I agree," said Bill Bardsley. "I can't believe that Dr. Clay put us up to this. It's scandalous, and I'm not hanging around any longer."

"Gentlemen, gentlemen, don't be so hasty," said a voice from behind. "Allow me to introduce myself. I'm Peter Shapely, professor of theology at Berkeley. I too am flabbergasted at the happenings we've just witnessed, but I will say this, I've known Dr. Clay for some twenty years, and he is not the type of person to waste anybody's time, especially not his own." The people around him remained silent as they considered what he said. Others joined the growing group and listened intently. "It's obvious to me that there's nothing contrived about any of this. Dr. Clay wouldn't go to that bother. He'd be the first to be embarrassed about it. No, that line of reasoning is not up for debate based on the man who organized all of this. Instead, we should focus on what's said. Let's all calm down and give due consideration to the objectives of this gathering, which I believe are to have open minds and hearts. Both Dr. Clay and Rapoe have said this a couple of times," he said, taking his seat.

"I think Peter is right," said theological professor, Lila Thompson, adding to the conversation. "I don't know Dr. Clay, as well as I know Peter, but what he says gives me every reason to discuss intelligently the things we've learned this evening."

"Makes sense to me," said Zapper. "Not that I'm an expert on anything scientific or theological, but as a member of the human race, I think that what we've heard is earth-shattering, and for that reason alone, I'm certainly hangin' around. You know what I'm sayin'?" he concluded, popping a piece of gum into his mouth.

"I'm with you, Zapper," said Lance. "Who are we to dismiss what could be true. We have to discuss all of this," he added.

"Maybe we should all take a little time out, have some coffee, visit a rest-room, as the general said, and then regroup inside in say fifteen minutes?" suggested Peter. Everybody nodded except Dan Rosenberg, who moved quickly away towards the podium. He climbed up on to the small stage and said,

"Excuse me, ladies and gentlemen. I am Rabbi Dan Rosenberg. I've listened to enough. I refuse to tread a path of heresy. If you feel like joining me, I suggest we talk with Dr. Clay immediately.

"We're both with you," said Bill Bardsley and astrophysicist Brian Kingston.

Dan waited another moment before leading the small group towards the armed officer guarding the door to the barracks. The officer adjusted his gun across his chest in a guarding action.

"We'd like to see Dr. Clay, now!" he barked, unintimidated by the officer's demeanor. At that moment the door opened -

"It's okay, officer. I'll deal with this," said Dr. Clay. "Please follow me," he said, moving across the floor towards a curtained off area where they found the general already seated at a table with five chairs. "Take a seat, everybody," added a smiling Dr. Clay, unmoved by their demeanor. Dan took the seat beside the general, while Bill Bardsley sat beside the general. The nurse wheeled Brian Kingston towards the table.

"I understand that you have concerns about what you have witnessed tonight and I believe you're representing this group, Dan," said Dr. Clay in a calm and controlled manner.

"I'm not anyone's representative, except for the one true God, not some electronic voice that you've invented. I'm disgusted and disappointed in you, Dr. Clay, for having the audacity to have these eminent people travel halfway across the world to witness some ego-built toy that we are supposed to worship. I'll say this - I for one will ensure that the world's media hears about this. Don't be surprised if you are publicly humiliated, because after this debacle you deserve to be," he said with vitriol supported by the other two.

"Does anybody else want to say something?" asked Dr. Clay. It was his arch-enemy, Brian Kingston who spoke next, saying -

"I agree with the Rabbi, but I'm not one to ridicule another, no matter how annoyed I might feel. So, let me say this - I am deeply disappointed in you, Dr. Clay. How could you possibly have imagined that somebody, or something, could appear like some Disney character, and make wild statements with your total support! I'm stunned, Dr. Clay - stunned, and bitterly disappointed. I will make sure that your reputation is damaged over this outrage. I demand to leave immediately."

"As do I, Dr. Clay," said Bill Bardlsey. "I've known of your work for many years, and I cannot believe you should stoop so low as to want us to support some ego trip to maintain your celebrity status." Dr. Clay realized where it was going and said,

"I'm sorry that you feel that way. I have nothing further to add that would make you want to change your mind. It wasn't my intention to mislead any of you in any way. The general and his staff have already made the necessary arrangements. You can leave immediately. Thank you for obliging us, and I apologize once again." The general stood up, saying,

"Your belongings have already been loaded onboard the aircraft. You will find the flight back to the States a lot more acceptable than your journey here. There will be food and more comfortable surroundings for each of you. Follow me," he said by way of an order rather than a request. The people were annoyed by his curtness, but decided to say nothing further and followed him.

Dr. Clay peeped through the curtains to see what was happening in the main hall. He was happy to see that the core of the group was still intact, and wasn't surprised that his arch-enemy, Brian Kingston, was one of the ones that wanted to go as he and Dr. Clay had never seen eye to eye over the years. He saw that two groups were forming; one consisted mainly of scientists and astrophysicists, while the other was a general mix that included ecclesiastics, philosophers, alongside Lance and Zapper.

"Dr. Clay, this lady would like to speak with you," said a uniformed officer from behind. Noel turned around to find the officer beside Brian Kingston's nurse. She was a slim brunette of medium height with a face that carried a pleasant smile.

"Certainly, what can I do for you?" he asked, noticing that the woman looked nervous and embarrassed.

"My name is Mary-Rose O'Connor. I'm Dr. Kingston's private nurse, or at least I was until I told him I wanted to stay. Can I stay - please?" she pleaded. Dr. Clay smiled and held her shoulders, saying,

"Of course you can. It is my pleasure that you want to be here with us. Did you find it, illuminating?" Her demeanor changed immediately to one of excitement.

"Oh, more than that. I think it's the most amazing moment of my life. I feel as if I've gone to heaven. Thank you, Dr. Clay. I won't be any bother," she said, hurrying off to join one of the groups. He smiled as he whispered, "Gone to heaven. I'd say you couldn't have put it any more perfectly, Mary-Rose."

    *   *   *   *

"It looks as if we are forming into two groups," said Edgar, looking at a bunch of people at the other end of the hall having a conversation. The other group seems to be comprised mainly of scientists, leaving the rest of us to fend for ourselves."

"May I join you," asked John Mahoney, moving towards a vacant chair next to Edgar. He introduced himself and shook the hands of those already seated.

"I'd like to join this group also? My name is Khalid, and I represent my Muslim people," he said, moving in beside John.

"Everybody's welcome to team up with whatever group they want," added Edgar.

"My name is, John Mahoney, papal advisor. It's my pleasure to make your acquaintance finally," he said, holding out his hand to Khalid.

"I am very pleased to meet with you. It's a pity your friend Mr. Rosenberg decided not to stay."

"Yes, I'm afraid it became a little too much for him to bear. What about you, what do you make of it all?" Khalid folded his hands as he thought about his answer.

"I am a broad-minded Muslim. I'm also a teacher to many of my people. Let me say that I won't be broadcasting what I see any time soon." Everybody smiled at the humor and thought about the paradox that confronted the Muslim leader.

"I think it would be prudent to elect a chairperson to run the discussion?" suggested Edgar.

"I'd say you're it," said Lance, and nobody objected.

"It would be a good idea if we went around the table and introduced ourselves. How about starting with you, Lance?" asked Edgar.

"No problem. Lance Wilde, movie star, and a guy who doesn't know why the hell he's here!" he said, while everybody chuckled.

"Next person," asked Edgar.

"Zapper Zee, but everybody calls me Zapper. It's great to be in the company of such intellectuals. Oh, I'm a musician."

"Lila Thompson, Professor of psychiatry at Cornell," announced Lila.

"Andrew Johnston, and I'm an astrophysicist. I know I should be at the other table, but I started with my good friends, Lance and Zapper, and that's where I'll stay," he said, glancing towards Lance and Zapper who acknowledged with a chuckle.

"John Mahoney, advisor to the Pope."

"Khalid, advisor to the Muslim people," he said, smiling at John.

"And what about you at the back?" asked Edgar, looking at the nurse. She blushed before answering,

"I'm sorry. My name is Mary-Rose O'Connor. I am - was Dr. Kingston's nurse."

"And I'm Edgar Snipes, philanthropist," he said, completing the formalities. Right then. Would anyone like to start?" There was a general silence as one person looked at another.

"I'm still trying to work out how I hear my voice," said Zapper. "It's more than cool. Do you know what I'm saying? How does he do that? It was as clear as a bell, and scary too,"

"At first, I thought the sounds we were hearing was an organized thing, but according to the general, the government has nothing to do with it, and besides, we were out in the night sky with no visible communications around. You hear yourself speaking all the time, and you never give it a second thought, but it's more than weird hearing your voice speaking back at you," added Lance.

"I think there were more earth-shattering moments than hearing our voices in our heads," added Lila Thompson.

"I agree, Lila, but Zapper and Lance have a point about being able to hear ourselves in our voices. Maybe Rapoe was trying to demonstrate that he could do it? I don't know. What were you about to say, Lila?" asked Edgar.

"The mere fact that something up there," she said, pointing upwards, "who purports to be God, tells us that he didn't create the earth - that he found it, is jaw-dropping in the extreme, but then to continue in that vein by announcing he didn't make us, is…well, mind-blowing!" she added.

"Totally," added Andrew. "I don't believe I would ever have contemplated this arising in any physics examination paper, or during my studies as an astrophysicist. It is beyond interesting."

"I wonder could we go around the table and ask this one pertinent question?" asked Edgar.

Everybody looked in his direction. "Do you believe that Rapoe is God?" he said. Everybody looked around and breathed out slowly, unsure of their answer and not wanting to be the first to give their opinion.

"I believe it," said a voice from the back. Everybody turned and looked at Mary-Rose. "I'll tell you why I believe he's God," she said, standing up. "Before I came here, I knew nothing about what was going to happen, nor knowing any of the people who were coming. My employer, Mr. Kingston, had expounded the virtues of Dr. Clay and told many people that he had never met a more brilliant mind in all of his seventy-five years on earth. I was so looking forward to seeing Dr. Clay, and I was not disappointed when I heard what he had to say. I did open my mind and was as shocked as everybody at what I've heard. Then, when my employer discarded everything and demanded to go home, I couldn't believe that his faith in Dr. Clay was that fickle. So, firstly, I believe in the gentleman that brought us all here, and I'm keen to hear his views. I, for one, know in my heart that we are listening to God. I know it's not very scientific, but it's all

I've got." She sat down as all eyes continued to stare at her.

"Thank you, Mary-Rose, and I have every reason to believe in you. I'm a natural skeptic, and I wish I had as open a mind and a heart as you," said Edgar. "Anyone else like to give an opinion?" he asked. "I'd like to think the same as Mary-Rose," said Lance. "You see, I've been thinking about what Rapoe said about having nothing to do with our creation. You know, it makes a lot of sense to me, and here's why. You know how people always pray to God when they need something, or when they are in desperate straits? Sometimes things get fixed, and he gets the credit. More times than not, he gets the blame for not fixing things. Well, if he claims he never made us and he's not present on earth, then that would make more sense to me. I also say it for another reason, one that's very personal." Lance looked down at the table and choked a little as he began to say, "I lost my daughter when she was aged seven. She was in a car accident being driven home from school when she got hit by some guy who was high on drugs. I prayed for 24 hours every day that God would make her better, but she never recovered. I never spoke to God or referred to him ever again. I became an atheist. If what we're all witnessing is true, then I for one would be happy to stop blaming God for something he couldn't fix. I hope he is God."

"And what about all the bad things that happen on our planet like earthquakes, floods, disasters?" added Zapper. "Look how hurricanes destroy the islands of the Caribbean and kill thousands, and make hundreds of thousands homeless. Surely a God would not put us on earth that would threaten us with all of these things? It makes sense to me, as Lance said, to want to believe that God didn't make us and I for one find that easier to believe." Edgar nodded to Zapper and acknowledged Lance's heart-rendering story. He allowed the words to sink in before asking, "I'd like to get a clerical input into all of this. We are fortunate to have amongst us, two of the world's foremost authorities in their respective faiths. Would either Khalid or John like to contribute to the conversation?" John looked at Khalid, who beckoned him to go first. John sighed deeply and rubbed his hand through his hair.

"Gosh, this is a tough one. I suppose I've dreamt all of my life about what I would say if I ever confronted God, and low and behold, he is supposedly in front of us. We preach that he is always around us, always loving us. I understand what Lance has said, and I am so sorry to hear of his great loss. But, there are lots of examples as to why God did create our world. Look at the beauty that surrounds us - our magnificent natural world full of awe and splendor, together with the awesomeness of our oceans. None of this happened by chance. Do the scientists deny that we are the only planet that happens to be the exact distance from our star that supports life; or that our perfectly positioned moon happens to be the correct distance and size between our earth and the sun that allows us to have tides and witness a total eclipse? As far as I am aware, we haven't found any other planet that supports life! Do they not ask themselves - why? I could go on, but everybody here can think of many more examples without my assistance. All I'm saying is that I, too, would like to hear from Dr. Clay before I could begin to give my opinion. I could not, and would not, venture an opinion on such a hugely important matter considering my education. I, like my friend Khalid, have studied all of the scriptures, including the Koran. We are men, whom a lot of people look to for guidance. It would be very remiss of both of us even to begin to admit that Rapoe is the Creator - is God! Science seeks to answer the questions of what and how. Theology seeks to answer the question of why and who - and ultimately of how. Our faith is that this vast universe was created by an omnipotent and boundlessly loving God, through Jesus Christ; that humanity is created in the image of God and is the pinnacle of his creation; and that we were created to live in communion with him. That is my feeble attempt to summarize what we believe. I can't prove it, but I believe it with all my heart. I'll leave it at that, but before this journey is over, I will, if you are still interested, give you my honest opinion before we depart this island."

"That's an honest statement, John. I'd say I speak for all of us that we respect your honesty," added Edgar.

"I would like to say that my esteemed colleague is right about one thing," added Khalid. "He says we cannot give an opinion on something so unbelievable until, and unless, we get much more substantial proof. I would not venture to discuss what I've heard with anybody, therefore, out of respect for my people, I remain open-minded as a human being, but closed as a Muslim."

"Can I say something?" added Zapper, to which Edgar smiled and nodded. "Like Mary-Rose, I'm no scientist, but if God didn't make us, then it makes sense to me for other reasons." Zapper licked his lips and stood. "Look at me! Look at this body of mine. It's bad. I'm fat, and I'm in pain most of the time. My father is only 60, and he's always got somethin' wrong with him. How many people do you know that have physical problems? Lots, I guess. Then you see how many people have to live with deformities, and are disabled for no other reason other than bad genes. Right? Well, Rapoe says he didn't make us, then that's fine by me because God is supposed to be all-powerful, all smart, and all-loving. A guy like that would have done a hell of a better job designing our bodies - if he had designed them. God would have made us withstand diseases and disfigurements. He would have made us a lot stronger. That's all I'm sayin'," he said, as he sat back down. People nodded, unable to dispute what Zapper had said. They'd never thought about it like that before.

"There seems to be a consensus that we'd all like to hear what Dr. Clay has to say. With your permission, I'll go and find him and ask him if he would do that?" said Edgar, leaving his seat and heading in the direction of the stage.

* * * *

The second group was involved in deep conversation when they were interrupted,

"May I join you all?" asked Peter Shapely.

"Please do, Peter," said Fred Pinkton, pointing to a chair.

"I know Fred is a physicist at NASA. But, I don't know either of you," said Peter, looking at the other two men.

"I'm Laurence Shelvey, astronomer and this is my colleague, Frank Dipple. We both work at the space center in Houston."

"I'm very pleased to make your acquaintance. So what have you been discussing?" asked Peter.

"You've probably gathered that the science fraternity knitted together, far away from the non-science factor, like oil and water never mixing," said Fred Pinkton. The two astronomers smiled.

"I can understand that, but I believe this may be one of those times when we'd better take another look at the chemistry that separates those two compounds. I don't think we can get away with one science, without discussing the other?" added Peter.

"Agreed, but we scientists are much more enthralled with the scientific aspect of what this Rapoe person is telling us," said Fred. "For example, he says that he didn't create our world, which we know to be true. Earth came about due to extraordinary circumstances and quite unbelievable coincidences. As you know, we wouldn't be here if not for the comet that destroyed the earth when it struck the Yucatan Peninsula some 40 million years ago, putting an end to the dinosaur era. Had that comet been a moment sooner or later, the dinosaurs, or some other creature, would now be in charge, and humanity would never have existed. If this Rapoe is God, then I'm a semi-believer due to his statement. We all want to ask him scientific questions concerning the big bang, our universe, and questions that abound about gravity, black holes, pulsars, …the list is endless. Indeed, he has shocked us all because we never had an agenda and we didn't know what to expect. I want to know about his relationship with Dr. Clay and how he happened to find our planet. All in all, it boils down to Dr. Clay giving us greater clarity. Wouldn't you agree?" he said to Peter and the group in general, who all nodded in agreement.

"Then let me locate Dr. Clay and put that to him," said Peter, rising from his seat, leaving the group to talk amongst themselves. The three men nodded their agreement leaving Peter to go in search of Dr. Clay. A moment or so later, Peter bumped into Edgar who was on the same mission.

"Looks like the two groups are of one mind," said Edgar.

"Yes, indeed. It looks like Dr. Clay will have to clarify many things before we can make any real headway," agreed Peter.

One of the officers told them that Dr. Clay was outside on the gantry up top. They grabbed some coffees and made their way up the winding metal stairs at the side of the building.

*   *   *   *

Dr. Clay hadn't been able to sleep. He stood leaning against the railing of the gantry looking across at the fading image of Rapoe against the sunlight and reckoned he had only managed about four hours sleep in the last twenty-four. Dr. Clay also saw that some of his guests were underneath the cloud looking up at Rapoe. He knew they'd be curious to know who or what was in there, but he also knew that they were wasting their time.

"I suppose you haven't slept properly since all of this occurred?" said a voice from behind. Dr. Clay turned and saw Peter and Edgar arriving with coffees. Dr. Clay took a coffee from him, saying -

"Thank you, Peter. I was thinking that very same thought," he said, sipping the hot coffee. They both watched Edgar take a small box from his pocket and pop a pill into his mouth.

"Are you feeling all right, Edgar," asked Dr. Clay.

"Couldn't be better. These new pills keep me awake. I need to keep my mind sharp with all that's going on. Would you like one?" asked Edgar. Peter shook his head negatively, as did Dr. Clay. Peter turned to Dr. Clay asking -

"I wondered if you are concerned about the uproar that will occur back on the mainland when you return? After all, I wouldn't imagine Rabbi Rosenberg will remain quiet when he gets back. He did say he was going to speak to the press!" Dr. Clay smiled, saying,

"I've no concerns in that regard whatsoever. Remember, Rapoe enabled us to hear ourselves in his words using our voices. He has ultimate control over what we hear and say. I know that Rapoe is quite capable of retaining our anonymity and protecting us from the likes of Dr. Rosenberg."

Peter was unsure what Dr. Clay was referring to when he said that Rapoe had control, but before he could take the discussion any further, Dr. Clay continued, saying - "But, you know, I'm relieved in one way that I managed to get it all out into the open arena. I feel like I'm no longer alone. A problem shared is a problem halved and all that." He took another sip of coffee and thoughtfully bit his lower lip before continuing, "I was thinking, before you arrived, about how the NASA New Horizons probe recently radioed back a strikingly clear photo of a small, icy world called Ultima Thule. It's one of the farthest we've ever identified, a staggering 6.5 billion kilometers from the earth; yet here before us stands a craft from the outer regions of our universe containing the word of God. It puts a whole new perspective on things, wouldn't you say?" Peter and

Edgar looked towards the vapor, thinking of Dr. Clay's comments, before he continued, saying, "There's a huge amount that I haven't revealed yet. Rapoe has agreed to divulge everything in his way, in his own time. Over the past year or so, we discussed and rehearsed everything we needed to say. I've been to this island about ten times." Edgar and Peter raised their eyebrows with surprise. Dr. Clay turned to them, asking, "How may I help you, Edgar and Peter?" They explained the circumstances leading up to their seeking him out.

"Why of course I'll explain everything," he said. "I intended to do just that. Let's gather everybody around, shall we?" Dr. Clay watched as the two men moved down the stairway, and wondered if he should have taken one of Edgar's pills after all?

*   *   *   *

Both Peter and Edgar gathered their respective groups into the center of the hall facing the podium. When everybody had settled, Dr. Clay started.

"I hope by now that you all understand the need for the paucity of information in my invitation." Most people nodded. "I have never had to experience anything like this. As I said before, Rapoe contacted me nearly two years ago, and it took me a very long time to understand and comprehend what was happening. I thought I was hallucinating. I sought therapy, but I was afraid to tell my therapist the truth. I couldn't even tell my wife, because I didn't think she'd understand. I became terrified. Rapoe was extra patient with me, and eventually, I calmed down and treated it as a great scientific problem. Since then, I concentrated all of my efforts towards this weekend's events. I didn't know what I was supposed to do? I had no clue as to whether any of you would turn up? I am so glad that you did. I had to be clandestine in my approach. There was no way any of you would have accepted an invitation that read - *'Hi all, would you like to come to a secluded island in the Pacific some weekend and meet God!?'* The audience smiled at the humor. "I didn't think so. Neither could I entrust what I had learned with anybody, and that included my wife, who thinks I'm at some boring seminar, being bored and annoying at the same time. At least I hope she's thinking that way! Let me try to explain things as I see them. First off, I'm an atheist!" The audience locked on to his every word and began to admire his honesty. "Sure, I was raised as a good christian, attended Sunday school, and did all the right things in my parent's eyes," he continued. "Then, I reached the age where science shoved everything aside, and I ended up pushing all other beliefs into a back room and locking the door. But I left the key in the lock - on the outside! I suppose religious teaching had done its job in making me fear the unknown and making me keep things on standby - just in case! I went about my career, and my life, oblivious in all respects to a Creator of anything - until now! I've always had respect for Darwinism and his theory of evolution. The science is getting closer all the time to proving our descendency. I also understand the point of view of atheists and agnostics. Science has disproven many of the legends about the birth of humanity and the creation of our earth." Dr. Clay paused momentarily, took a sip of water, and continued, "I have always been fascinated by astrophysics. It is my life's passion. I never cease to be amazed at our discovery successes. Look how we've sent our probes to planets within our solar system, and landed a craft on the Moon and Mars! Back in 1977, we sent Voyagers 1 and 2 on their incredible journeys. Look at the vast riches of the universe that Hubble has shown us! We are learning more in one year that humanity couldn't learn in 2000 years. And we never stop advancing in our search for knowledge. We will soon witness the launch of the Webb observatory that will be sent over a million miles out into space to observe what we have never seen before. How exciting is that? It's incredible! Amazing!" he said, pausing for effect. "And today, you are witnessing something much more incredible - much more amazing than everything else we've learned." Dr. Clay pointed towards the outside of the building, saying - "Rapoe came to me because of my fame, and possibly because he trusts me. I hope the latter is true." Dr. Clay took the bottle of water and drank half of it. He knew what he was about to say, and it scared him to death. He swallowed hard and looked deep into the audience, saying -

"Yes, I do believe in him. I do believe that he is the God we heard and read about; the God we fear;

the God that most of the world loves!" The audience broke into conversation immediately. Edgar and Peter looked at one another with surprise that Dr. Clay was so genuinely audacious. John Mahoney could barely control himself, realizing that Dr. Clay had just put his reputation on the line. Even Khalid sat upright in his chair and looked around to ensure he didn't imagine what he'd just heard. The scientists, astrophysicists, and philosophers sat back amazed that a man of the caliber and high esteem of Dr. Clay could make such a statement. Dr. Clay smiled and raised his hands appealing for quiet. "Yes, I know, it's shocking. Why would a man who has done so much to dispute the perceived origins of man; someone who has published books, and made numerous TV series proclaiming the wonders of our universe without a God, suddenly deem that he is now a believer? There is nobody more surprised at these statements than the person who is speaking to you now." He drank some more water, finishing off the bottle. The sweat was oozing from his body, knowing what he'd just said. There was no going back now. He had made a bold and brave statement; now, it was up to Rapoe to support his assertions. General Blenfold touched Dr. Clay's arm, gently whispering, "I think it would be sensible to let me take over from here." Dr. Clay was surprised at the general's intervention but happy to allow him to do so. Dr. Clay took a step backward, leaving the general to face the audience.

"It is now nearly dawn. I would strongly suggest that we all get some rest. It's been a long night, and we have a lot to consider. We all need to regroup and address these things later this morning. I would suggest we get together at ten hundred hours. Breakfast will be available at that time," said General Blenfold, more by way of an order than a request. He nodded to Dr. Clay, who appeared exhausted and happy that the general had taken control of matters. The attendees muttered among themselves, looking dazed and confused. John Mahoney and Khalid shook their heads in unison, not knowing what to do or say, as this was way beyond both their expectations.

"I think I need some time alone to try and make sense of what we've witnessed," said John to Khalid.

"I agree. My mind is swirling with thoughts and questions. I bid you goodnight, until the morning," replied Khalid, making his way to the sleeping area.

"This beats any Oscar-winning performance I've ever known. I only wish I could tell the outside world what's going on," said Lance, staring up at the image outside that was Rapoe.

"Oh man, this is like some crazy trip," added Zapper. "I'm zonked, man. I'm gonna get some big-time 'Zapper Z' s,'" he reiterated and headed towards the washrooms. He passed Mary-Rose and bid her goodnight, but she was transfixed by the side of a bunk bed whispering some quiet prayers. Peter and Edgar remained seated by the window, peering out at the vapor image before them.

"Where do you think this is all going to go?" asked Peter. Edgar looked through the window as the vapor began to deflect into the dawn, making it harder to see.

"Beats me, Peter. I hope that Dr. Clay is okay and that he hasn't over-extended himself. He looks slightly exasperated. I'm worried for him," he concluded.

"I agree. We should keep a close eye on him and help him out whenever the need arises. Come on, let's do as the general commanded and get some shut-eye."

Lila, Andrew Johnston, and all of the scientific invitees were already finishing off their snacks and making their way to their bunks.

The general looked down from a high vantage point on the gantry and could sense their confusion. He also knew that he had to take control of matters when he did. His experience told him that this group could get out of control at any minute. He needed to be somebody who showed authority as Dr. Clay was way too much involved in the whole process to notice such things, and he was concerned that Dr. Clay might not be able to achieve what he set out to do. He would have to maintain strict control over proceedings until this weekend was over. The general looked out the top window and saw that the Rapoe vehicle was disappearing into the dawn background and would be invisible very shortly. His one wish was that he could have captured the vapor and investigated what made it travel. They had tracked it on the three previous visits when Dr. Clay and Rapoe were discussing and rehearsing what they should say and do. They were all baffled by the speed at which it appeared and disappeared. It seemed to be faster than the speed of light - which was impossible! The satellites managed to track the vapor on each of its exits, but for some unknown reason, it disappeared each time within seconds of take-off leaving no trail or omission. None of his top technical teams could fathom it. Even the NASA scientists were baffled. They had used everything available to them to try and determine its construction without success. It was unlike anything they had come across before. The general had studied their findings and understood their exasperation. The general concluded that Rapoe was some extraterrestrial being. As to whether it was God was another matter, and not for his consumption. When the top brass asked him for his assessment, he would classify it as a UFO of no material consequence.

Chapter Six.

The night moved quickly. Most people had been unable to sleep, while a few had managed a couple of hours. Once everybody had taken their first coffees and freshened up after taking a shower, they all made their way outside into the sun, and eagerly awaited the arrival of Dr. Clay.

"When I awoke this morning, I thought it had all been a dream until I looked around and saw everybody," said John Mahoney to Khalid.

"Dr. Clay did tell us that we wouldn't be disappointed; however, I'm not sure if we are all not wasting our time," replied Khalid.

"Where's Rapoe?" asked Mary-Rose, looking towards the sky. Other people had been wondering the same thing and searched the skies.

"I don't know about anybody else, but I never shut an eye," said Zapper, yawning and looking around.

"Me neither," said Lance. "I guess the adrenaline is pumping within us at a rate of knots."

"Good morning everybody," said Dr. Clay, taking to the podium. "I trust everybody is well rested and eager to move along?" he asked, noticing almost all heads had nodded positively. "I know that what you have witnessed is beyond anybody's comprehension. Rest assured that I understand how you must be feeling right now. I've had nearly two years to go through what you've experienced in only a few hours. It's been a titanic struggle for me getting to this stage and sharing it with all of you. Before all of this happened, I assumed that I would have continued with my scientific and personal life, never imagining that the answers to all of my studies would happen in one fell swoop. Rapoe has shattered all of our illusions by revealing that he didn't create our planet or had any hand in creating us. How unbelievably astounding is that? When you think about it, it makes a lot of sense. It gets rid of a lot of obstacles that have hindered humanity for thousands of years. For the first time, we are learning the truth about our existence. We are also privileged to be the first people to know that there is the possibility of an afterlife for those of us who want it." Dr. Clay paused as he thought about his words.

His audience could see that he was speaking earnestly and had no pre-prepared script. "I, for one, want it more than anything. But, that's not the reason for my contention that Rapoe is God. He has shown me many things that he is about to disclose to you as well. I repeat you must open your hearts and minds to what you are about to learn. Allow me to begin by inviting Rapoe back amongst us." Dr. Clay put his fingers to his temples and looked up to where Rapoe had appeared before. This time, people remained seated and showed no anxiety, now that the first mystery had worn off. A moment later, there were a flurry of cloud roughly 20 feet in the air with a piercing light at its center. The audience waited with bated breath, not knowing what to expect.

"Rapoe, thank you for appearing. As you can see, we have lost a number of our guests; however, I'm happy to say that the majority are still here," said Dr. Clay, unsure what Rapoe was going to say next. The audience was startled once again by the sound of their voices inside their heads speaking someone else's words, as Rapoe said -

"Dr. Clay has put his career in jeopardy for my sake. I will always thank him for that. There have been many great men in the past who have done the same. I have already mentioned Moses, Isaiah, and Joshua, but, there were many more who assisted me that have never received any mention or accolade for the great work they did on my behalf. I also thank all of you for your bravery in remaining. I know it has not been easy for any of you. A stranger arrives from an unknown place and tells you He is your God, is not something that rests easily. I understand all of that. Many of you have never believed in me, and some of you are devoted to me. A lot of you are scientists who tend to only believe in your respective sciences, never wanting to imagine that someone like me existed. I understand all of that, as well. The God that you have studied; the God you think you know about, is not me! The early scribes wrote what they heard and saw. They also wrote what they were ordered to write, sometimes on pain of death. These evil men used what the prophets proclaimed for their purposes. They abused their positions for their greed, and the people were the ones who suffered. They painted a picture of me as someone to fear; someone who would damn you to the fires of hell if you didn't obey my commandments. I am not that God. I am not the God that wants to harm you: I am the God that loves you. I am not the God that you should fear; I am the God that will protect you: I am not the God that will reject you: I am the God that will welcome you and give you eternal life." The audience remained captivated by his words. Here was a supposed God that didn't sound like the God that they were conditioned to believe. Here was someone who was telling them the truth about Himself. Everybody remained stationary as they gazed at the light. Dr. Clay looked down at them from the podium and knew that they were truly engaged. Even the general appeared to be distracted as he too listened intently. Rapoe continued -

"I know I asked a lot from humanity to believe in me when there were so many unanswered questions. But these questions only arose over time. Many thousands of years ago, the people who inhabited your earth were not capable of thinking the way that you do. They worshipped the stars and many false prophets. It was only through the intercession of the great men I've mentioned that humanity began to listen and to wonder. Their belief became one built out of fear, which was not something that I wanted. I wanted them to love me, but I knew that it would take a long time. Now, we are at a time when humanity has come to understand much more than they did back then. You think that you can control your destiny without any God - without Me! I can assure you that this is not the case. There is no other god, but me! In the billions of years, before you existed, I searched the universe and found no other being. The reason for this is quite simple. You have learned how your planet came about by a series of circumstances and good fortune. You are also learning how you yourselves were created, again, by extraordinary and unique occurrences. It was no different for us. We evolved too. We didn't have to go through any changes to our existence, in the same way, that you did. There were no asteroids to destroy us and no volcanic eruptions. There were no other creatures that inhabited us. We were the first. It meant we had a peaceful creation, and we used that good fortune to enhance ourselves intellectually. We didn't have any of the human conditions, such as emotions, or hate. We did have one thing in common. We both had love. My kingdom nurtured that love, whereas you destroyed it." The audience were shocked at what they'd just heard. The scientists amongst them jumped up excitedly saying,

"I knew there was no Creator. Now we hear it from the horse's mouth," shouted Frank Dipple, the astronomer.

"So you're saying that you believe what Rapoe is telling us?" asked Fred Pinkton, the NASA physicist.

"Yes. You heard it for yourself," replied Frank.

"Then you believe that Rapoe exists. That He is God!" answered Fred. Frank Dipple didn't know what to say. Instead, he sat back down, quietly pondering his words.

"I like his honesty," added Edgar Snipes, breaking the silence. "Here we have our supposed God telling us that we have nothing to fear from him and that He too was created, just like us, albeit with a greater intellect. I see nothing wrong with any of this," he announced to a spellbound audience. Dr. Clay allowed the comments to continue, before saying -

"Rapoe, please continue." Then Rapoe said -

"I was made in the same way as you, by a series of chemical reactions many billions of years ago, in another world, in a different part of the universe. You have learned that all planets have a finite life, especially your own. Your planet is halfway through its life. You can prolong your planet's life, and I believe you already know how to do that. If you don't, then you will be doing the inhabitants of the future a disservice. Your planet is all that you've got. There are no alien planets available to you that you can reach. You have no craft that would enable you to achieve that. No energy source in the universe will provide the fuel you'd need to travel to distant worlds. Yes, there are many such worlds. I have found many millions of planets that give life. Unfortunately, most of those planets are not the welcoming sort. Some worlds have creatures that have even amazed me! It's rare to come across a planet with living intelligent beings like you. Many frightening planets are enormous, some millions of times the size of the earth. One such planet is My kingdom." A mixture of sounds greeted his words.

"Wow!" said an excited Zapper.

"If this doesn't beat anything, then nothing will," added Lance.

"This is quite extraordinary," said Andrew, crossing and uncrossing his legs unable to get comfortable. "I wouldn't have believed it if I hadn't heard it for myself," muttered Lila, gazing at the cloud. Rapoe continued, saying -

"So, you see, there cannot be any other God but me. I am here to save you. I am here to love you for all eternity." With those words, the audience broke into gasps of disbelief. The scientists and astrophysicists could barely contain themselves. They jumped to their feet, discussing with one another what was said, trying to analyze the content and make sense of what they'd heard. Rapoe remained quiet during the commotion. John and Khalid were disturbed. Khalid said;

"I think that this event is becoming unmanageable in my eyes. This Rapoe is now asking us to accept that everything we have learned is wrong. I cannot justify any of this. I feel duty-bound to leave. I'm afraid I will have to take such an action, my friend." Khalid rose from his seat, and just as he turned to go, John grabbed his tunic, saying -

"I can appreciate your concerns, Khalid, and I understand this must seem very difficult for you as it is for me. Could you not divorce yourself from what is being said and perhaps not be a judge, but be an observer. I would feel happier knowing that another man of the cloth was in attendance. After all, there will probably be even greater revelations to come, and then we may all sit back and laugh about it all. I'm not taking it too seriously, myself."

"I'm sorry, my friend, but I have reached the limit of my endurance. Goodbye, until we meet again," was all Khalid said, making his way towards the end of the building. Dr. Clay noticed immediately and hoped nobody else would leave. He looked towards the general and found he was already moving towards the back of the building to ensure the safe departure of Khalid.

"He said *'his people,'* does that mean there are people on his planet - in this so-called heaven?" asked Edgar. Peter shook his head from side to side, saying -

"I have simply no idea. He also said there are many millions of planets, and he's seen them all! Wow, this gets more bizarre by the minute. Hold on, and I think someone's about to speak."

"Can I ask a question?" shouted Fred Pinkton, the NASA physicist, standing in the middle of the crowd. Dr. Clay put his fingers to his temple and looked towards Rapoe. A few seconds later, he turned to Fred, saying -

"Go ahead, Dr. Pinkton. Rapoe will answer your question.

"What we are hearing is astounding. It raises many questions, and I trust we will have the opportunity to ask those questions later. In the meantime, I believe everybody here would like to know the answer to one such question, and that is; How are you able to travel around a vast universe at such astonishing speeds? After all, even if you can travel at the speed of light, it would take you longer than billions of years to have seen the millions of planets you claim to have seen.?" he asked, as he sat back down. The rest of the people looked towards the light, wondering what Rapoe would say. They didn't have long to wait for an answer, as Rapoe said,

"I don't travel. I don't need to. Besides, I would be unable to do so for the same reasons that you have found. Let me explain. My kingdom existed long before yours, in a deserted part of the universe away from any galaxy. We have a star that is proportionately distant from our planet. There are no other planets near to us; therefore, we have no galactic threats to our existence. As I said before, we have no physicality. We don't need any. We developed with a very high intellect much greater than yours. We used that intellect to do away with the need for any physical presence. Our presence is our soul! The soul is the most powerful influence ever devised. It gives everything and never takes anything away. It allows us to be anywhere we want to be. We are in control of our souls, unlike you. It allows us to enter your minds as I am doing now. You will never have our capabilities until you join us. To do that you must prove yourselves worthy. I think it's important to explain what I mean by the soul. It is an intangible part of you. To find it, you must become aware of yourself through your mind. You must be able to control your mind and not let it control you. Only then will you be able to find your soul. Your soul is all-powerful and can lead you to eternal life. The innocents who have died and gone before you are already with me. The soul lives forever." The audience looked at one another and wondered about the audacious statements they were hearing. The skeptics amongst them became more skeptical, while the others hung on to His every word. Rapoe continued,

"I located your star and your earth just after it's creation. I had found many star systems that showed promise, but none that was equal to your solar system. I saw your earth being destroyed many times through ice-ages and volcanic destructions. Numerous asteroids hit it over millennia. Somehow, your earth survived. When I visited again some 50 million years ago, I saw that dinosaurs ruled it. They were frightening creatures which I'd seen on one other planet millions of years before.

Sometime after that, an asteroid crashed into your planet and caused it to become frozen. Another few million years later, your planet became what you see today. I was surprised to find some creatures had survived, and I was hopeful that maybe it would amount to something. For many millions of years, I have searched the universe looking to find souls that would join me in my kingdom. It was a fruitless exercise in most cases, but now and again, there was hope. When I revisited your earth, I was surprised to find many new creatures existed where none had been before. I observed over the years, and some 200,000 years ago, I saw the first examples of prehistoric man. It was only then that I knew I had found something special. I have been with you ever since, and watched how you have become what you are today." Rapoe paused for a moment, allowing his words to dwell in everybody's mind before continuing - "The universe is a strange and dangerous place. It is unpredictable, and it is a foolish man who thinks he can become its ruler. The universe can destroy you in an instant. I have witnessed the destruction of many newborn stars together with their neighboring planets. In our case, we knew almost immediately that we would have to rid ourselves of our physicality and become our non-destructive souls. That's when we found our souls. It is important that you too find your soul. I can help you do that. In that way, at the end of your life, you will be able to join me, providing you lead a good life by doing what I say." Again, the audience was taken aback with what they were hearing. They all looked towards Dr. Clay to see if he was taking things seriously. They didn't need any clarification on that thought when they saw how concentrated he was.

"My kingdom is a loving one. There is never any violence because we see the futility of such an act. Many times I have been saddened by the violence I have witnessed by the people of your earth. We found our souls at a very early stage in our development. Our one dream was to find new souls, hopefully. Your earth and one other were the only candidates that could fulfill our dream. We need new souls to inhabit my kingdom. That is the background of our creation." A long pause ensued, and the audience wondered had Rapoe finished speaking? Again, they looked towards Dr. Clay, who appeared unmoved by the silence. A hand went up in the audience, and Dr. Clay smiled as he said,

"Mary-Rose. What would you like to ask?" Mary-Rose looked more confident now as she said,

"Excuse me. I want to ask God what heaven is like?" People looked around at one another and thought that it was a question they had thought about, but were too embarrassed to ask. Andrew Johnston squeezed Mary-Rose's hand, saying -

"Well done, Mary-Rose. It's a wonderful question." She smiled back at him while Rapoe continued.

"Imagine a place that is free from sickness and pain! A place filled with love, happiness, and wonder! Where your life is unlimited, and you know no sadness - only joy; no weakness - only strength; no doubt - only belief. A place where there is no disappointment. Heaven is all of these things. Only the soul that follows my way will gain entry and join the legions of other souls who already enjoy my kingdom." Rapoe remained quiet while he allowed these images to cross people's minds. Then he continued, saying, "The life you lead here on earth is not the life you'll experience in heaven. You won't need memories or emotions, because there is nothing in heaven that requires them. Heaven does not require your bodies and your minds." Again, Rapoe paused and said nothing until he heard Mary-Rose asking,

"Can you show us heaven?"

"Wow, that's gutsy," whispered Fred Pinkton.

"I cannot show you my kingdom because your souls are not worthy," was all that Rapoe said. At that moment, Dr. Clay got up from his chair and announced,

"At this point, ladies and gentlemen, I would like us to pause and consider everything Rapoe has said - all of which has been a revelation to all of us. We need to take stock before we go on any further. Rapoe has suggested to me that this is what we should do. With that in mind, can I ask all of you to take a break, freshen up, and have something to eat? The general and his team have prepared something on your behalf inside the main building. It's now midday. May I suggest that after your lunch, we gather around as one group and discuss everything we've heard? I will take the chair.

Let's say 2 pm, inside the building out of the sun. Thank you all," he said, as he turned to the general, while everybody looked confused and exhausted by what they'd heard.

"I believe you've made the correct call by taking a break at this juncture, Dr. Clay," said the general. "I have to admit, doctor, that when I read the mission brief, I took it on because of your reputation. Having listened to Rapoe, I can see he speaks with authority. He's not a fraud," he said, dismissing himself and summoning two of his officers to accompany him. Dr. Clay smiled as he watched the general bark an order to his men. *"I suppose that's as good as anyone gets from the general,"* he thought, shuffling away from his guests to a secluded place he had reserved for himself. Dr. Clay needed a few hours rest, now that most things were out in the open. He had barely finished thinking the thought when his eyes closed, and he fell into a deep sleep.

*   *   *   *

"If anyone had told me that I would witness what I've witnessed this past 24 hours, I would have had them locked up," announced Lance to Zapper as they joined the others inside the main building. They were surprised to find two officers dressed in chef's aprons alongside two long tables filled with an array of buffet-style food.

"This is more like it," said Zapper, grabbing a plate and loading it with everything he saw.

Peter Shapely was doing the same thing when he noticed Mary-Rose in a corner looking forlorn. He grabbed a second plate and made his way over to her.

"I brought you some food, Mary-Rose. You ought to eat something," he said, placing the plate on the table beside her. "Would you like me to get you something to drink?" he asked.

"No, I'm fine, but thank you anyway."

"You look sad. Would you like to talk about it?" asked Peter, quietly eating some of the food. Mary's eyes were moist as she said,

"I was thinking how my life up to this point has been one without drama; then I arrive at this place and experience something so spectacular, it makes everything else that's happened in my life seem meaningless." Peter remained quiet as he waited for Mary-Rose to continue. She turned to him saying, "It makes you realize that the most important thing about this life - is the next!" she said, moving some food around on her plate with her fork.

"I suppose you're right about that, Mary-Rose. I feel the same way," he said, which made her look at him with surprise. He nodded, saying - "Yes, me too. We all become engrossed in our lives to the detriment of everything and everybody around us, and I'm no different. I guess we all need time to re-boot now and then. But, don't believe everything you've seen here. Remember, we have been listening to a voice that has made amazing statements, none of which are proven. Let's follow Dr. Clay's advice and sit down and discuss it. In the meantime, enjoy your food and keep an open mind." She smiled and tinkered with her food. Peter decided to leave her alone with her thoughts.

"I'm still wondering why we're here, Zapper?" said Lance. "I mean, the rest of these people, apart from Mary-Rose over there, are all highly qualified to attend something like this, but you and me, we're just your normal mega-music and movie stars!" He finished by chuckling at his comment but being serious at the same time.

"I think it has somethin' to do with us being famous. How many followers you got on social media?" asked Zapper. Lance thought about it saying -

"Somewhere around 3-400 million. Something like that. Why do you ask?"

"My number's closer to the billion, between You-Tube listens, Instagram, and all the rest of that stuff. I'm thinkin' that if we become followers of this Rapoe, they'd want us to use our pullin' power to bring in the brothers. You hear what I'm sayin'?" Lance remained silent as he considered Zapper's words. Then he added -

"You know; I think you have a point. It's the only thing that makes any sense. Anyway, I don't care. I'm just glad to be here. What we're hearing is earth-shattering. Even the scientists are amazed."

"Yeh, but my point is, how the hell are we supposed to start preachin' to people? I mean, I'm no apostle, and I don't think my fans would take anything I say seriously," added Zapper looking worried.

Everybody's mind concentrated on how the world was going to react when it learned of the events of this weekend. Peter Shapely sensed the trepidation, even amongst the scientists, and he wondered which of them were going to be the first to break the ranks and start supporting Dr. Clay?

Chapter Seven.

Dr. Clay waited until all were seated. He wanted a calm environment for everybody to contribute to the discussion. He asked the general to take his officers outside so that nobody would feel uncomfortable. He then cleared his throat, saying;

"I hope you enjoyed your food and gave yourself some alone-time to consider what we have heard. What we are witnessing this weekend is nothing short of mesmeric! What other words could adequately describe a situation where everything we thought we knew is being rewritten, from both a scientific and a spiritual perspective." He allowed his words to penetrate people's minds before continuing. "I would like to start this discussion by asking people to raise their hands if they believe that Rapoe is God!" People turned to one another to see who was going to raise their hand. The first to do so was Dr. Clay, which didn't come as a significant surprise. It took another thirty seconds or so before Mary-Rose raised her hand tentatively. Nobody else followed, so he continued - "I have made a list of points and grouped them into two parts - scientific and spiritual. I believe that the scientists amongst us will bear with me while I try to explain the background to our knowledge thus far." Peter, Andrew, and Fred Pinkton nodded their agreement. Dr. Clay looked around the group saying -

"I never cease to be amazed at man's ingenuity for discovery. Ever since Aristotle, Galileo, Newton, and Einstein laid the foundations, man has become unstoppable. We sent Voyagers 1 and 2 to explore deep space back in 1977, a journey that took twelve years to reach Neptune - the outermost planet in our solar system. Voyager continued its journey past Pluto, discovering the Kuiper Belt, some 4 billion miles away, astounding the scientists with the information they could only once imagine. Then came Hubble and look at the revelations that it unfolded! We learned that there are countless galaxies, possibly billions, and who knows how many stars and planets? The scale is beyond our wildest imaginations. We've landed a craft on Mars, Venus, and a moon of Saturn. The sciences of geology and archeology, together with Hubble, have allowed us to accurately calculate the ages of rocks, planets, and the universe." He paused, looking at each member of the group, as he said - "Then in one short weekend, we learn from Rapoe that Heaven is an enormous planet at the outer reaches of the universe; that he knows of millions of planets like ours, and that he can visit any of them in an instant. In hindsight, perhaps the word 'mesmeric' is not a big enough word. That is an excellent place to open the discussion to the floor. Let me start by asking the scientists amongst us about space travel. Would anyone like to comment about Rapoe's statement that he can travel anywhere in an instant, and explain it in such a way that the non-scientists amongst us could easily understand?

"I'd like to take this one," said Andrew Johnston. "I'm an astrophysicist like Dr. Clay. Rapoe wants us to believe that he can time-warp his way through space. Let me explain where humanity is concerning space travel. The early rockets of the 1960s, including Apollo 11, traveled at around 20,000 miles per hour. The Apollo 10 astronauts still hold the record for the fastest vehicle speed at around 24,000 miles per hour. We've since developed probes that can travel at around 150,000 miles per hour. The International Space Station travels at 17,500 miles per hour. None of these speeds would get us anywhere close to any planet in a reasonable time scale. For example, our nearest star is a small group called Alpha Centauri. It's approximately 4.37 light-years away. To put that into perspective, if we were to leave now, it would take us over 100,000 years to reach Alpha Centauri. And that's our nearest star-neighbor!" he said, pausing for effect. He could see that Lance, Zapper, John, and the other non-scientists were keenly interested in what he had to say. He continued, saying - "So, knowing that it can take that long to reach our nearest neighbor, it's safe to assume that we can forget about traveling any further into our galaxy, let alone any of the billions of other galaxies in the known universe. We would have to, at the very least, be able to travel at the speed of light if we were ever to hope of getting anywhere in a reasonable time." Andrew took a drink of water, smacked his lips together and continued, saying - "Here's what we mean by traveling at the speed of light. We would need to have the ability to do so at 186,000 miles per second, which means being able to circumnavigate the globe over seven times per second! Yes, ladies and gentlemen, I said seven times per second! There is no speed faster than the speed of light. No energy in the universe would give us that capability. That's where a man reaches a dead end. But that's not all! Our frail biology holds us back. The International Space Station allows us to conduct experiments on how to remain healthy in space. We have no idea how long-term space travel would affect us? We are only at the initial research stage. Rapoe tells us that not only can he travel at the speed of light - he can travel even faster! I would consider it scandalous for anybody to make such an assertion," said Andrew, raising his voice contemptuously. "I hope that gives you some idea about the vastness of space and the enormous barriers we encounter with space exploration and why, I for one, don't believe a word of what I've heard." Andrew finished his water while people discussed what he had said. Dr. Clay allowed the group a few minutes to themselves before saying -

"Andrew makes some valuable points, most of which are correct. He has factually outlined the problems concerning space exploration for which I thank him. Bear in mind, Andrew, that Rapoe is saying that He uses his soul to travel, otherwise he would have experienced the same difficulties as us. Now, I don't know very much, if anything, about the soul. All I know is what I learned in Sunday school. Rapoe also says that the soul's power is beyond our understanding. I believe that's what he said," said Dr. Clay, looking around, seeing most of his audience agreeing with his words. "I understand that the soul is different from the body and something that is for the afterlife. I believe that's correct, John," he asked, looking towards John Mahoney, who stood up saying,

"The church believes that God created the soul, which is imperishable. It is an intrinsic part of our faith. It's intangible in the same way that love is something that cannot be seen or grasped. It all ties down to a belief. If you know how to love, then you should also be able to find your soul," he said, as he sat back down.

"Thank you, John. As I was saying, Rapoe says that the soul is all-powerful and enables Him, not just to traverse the universe, but also to invade our minds. I believe he demonstrated this to us by allowing us to hear Him through our voices. I am not trying to defend Rapoe. I am trying to make sense of everything we are witnessing. He contacted me in the same way. You may have noticed that I put my fingers to my temple from time to time?" he said, as people nodded.

"Yes, I noticed that you do it every time you are about to speak to Rapoe," added Lance.

"It's the way he instructed me. I do it whenever I need to get in touch. I can't speak with him other than by speaking in a normal way." Dr. Clay looked around his audience and saw that everybody listened intently to what he was saying. He felt that this was the moment to shock them further. "To further clarify what Rapoe has said about the power of the soul, I must point out that the vision you see outside this building is not Rapoe. It's a representation of His presence!" With that, people stood up and rushed towards the windows. They could still see the cloud and couldn't understand why Dr. Clay had said it wasn't Rapoe.

"If you just remain seated, I'll explain further," he said, as they made their way slowly back to their chairs. "That mist, vapor, cloud, call it what you will, is not Rapoe. He created that image to give our brains a point of contact — something with which to focus. Rapoe is in his kingdom. In his Heaven!" he concluded, as he waited for a reaction.

"But how? That's impossible, Dr. Clay," said a now-standing Laurence Shelvey alongside an affronted Fred Pinkton. Please show us some respect, Dr. Clay," they insisted. Dr. Clay raised his arms slowly appealing for quiet.

"I know how this must sound to you, but if you'd let me explain further, you'll understand why I'm saying it." He waited for calm to return to the proceedings before continuing. "Rapoe is transmitting his messages to me and conversing with me from across the universe. How far, I do not know. He learned many billions of years ago that any biology would make space travel impossible. He found his soul, which enabled Him to abandon any form of travel and still have instant access to the universe. That's how God exists. That's why there is such a thing as God. That's why Rapoe is God!" There was no outburst this time at the mention of Rapoe being God.

"So, you're saying that he doesn't have to travel because he is a soul who can telepathically transmit visually and verbally. Is that correct?" asked astronomer, Laurence Shelvey. Dr. Clay breathed in deeply, knowing what was to come.

"I wouldn't say it's a form of telepathy, in the way that we understand. We categorize telepathy as a 'pseudo-science.' There is nothing spurious about what we are witnessing, so I would refer to Rapoe's ability as a form of transmittance that we don't understand.

"Preposterous," said Fred Pinkton. "There is no available science that says that can be possible. Where is this *soul* you're talking about?"

"I'm afraid that's where you're wrong," interrupted John Mahoney. "In Judeo-Christianity, only human beings have immortal souls. Other religions, like Hinduism, hold that all living things are the souls themselves. The soul is the incorporeal essence of a living being. It is not composed of matter and has no material existence, which makes it unexplainable just like love." People couldn't dispute the accuracy of what John had just explained. Dr. Clay asked -

"Who would like to raise a question, keeping it within the scientific arena?" Dr. Lila Thompson raised her hand saying -

"I am not a scientist. I am a theological philosopher. Could somebody tell me how Rapoe's planet could be many times the size of our earth?" It was Fred Pinkton who decided to answer.

"We haven't discovered anything as large as that. Within our solar system, Jupiter is 11 times larger than earth. Remember, Jupiter is a gas planet. The largest known rock planet discovered is Kepler-10c, which is around 17 times bigger than earth. However, the earth can fit into our sun some1.3 million times, and our sun is tiny compared to billions, if not trillions, of stars. So, I suppose there may be mega-sized planets such as Rapoes. What intrigues me is attempting to estimate the size of the star that supports such a planet!" he said, scribbling down some numbers on his writing pad.

"Therefore, a planet such as Rapoes could exist?" asked Lila, in a demanding tone. Dr. Clay looked at Fred Pinkton, wondering how he was going to answer. Fred Pinkton said,

"I wouldn't say such a planet couldn't exist, only…"

"That's all I wanted to know," interrupted Lila, satisfied that she got the answer she needed which started a general conversation within the rest of the group.

"I cannot imagine a planet that size. What about other planets?" asked Lance, directing his question at the group. "Rapoe says that he's seen all the other planets and yet only found two others that could sustain life, and one of those was earth. Is it possible that, of all the trillions of planets, that only two could be habitable?"

"That's a great question," responded Dr. Clay. "Perhaps I can assist on this one," said Andrew Johnston. Allow me to try to enlighten you if I can. There are countless planets in the universe. That much we know. Earth is in what we call the 'Goldilocks' zone; a planet that's not too far and not too near its mother star. As we've examined the universe using the observatories here on earth, such as the powerful Keck telescope in Hawaii, and especially using Hubble, we have found only a handful that might fall into that category, but I wouldn't hold my breath. As Rapoe has said, our earth came about because of a string of quite extraordinary circumstances. Therefore, it is logical to conclude that such events are infrequent." Dr. Clay continued where Andrew finished, saying -

"Thank you, Andrew. The problem is, as Rapoe has said, such a planet that supports life may already have inhabitants that would not be of the welcoming kind. We believe that for intelligent life to exist requires a planet that has the right blend of chemicals, especially oxygen. The vast majority of planets wouldn't have that magical composition of minerals and gases. Which brings us neatly to the other topic that needs discussing, and that is the spiritual one. Dr. Clay studied the notes he had made prior to bringing up the current topic.

"I have to say, this whole thing is enthralling," said John Mahoney to Edgar, as they waited for Dr. Clay to continue the discussion.

"You should be particularly looking forward to the next session," added Edgar.

"Yes, absolutely, but I have an avid interest in the cosmos. What we are learning from Rapoe about his method of travel, and the size of his kingdom is breath-taking."

"You mean his planet?" added Edgar, to which John smiled, not having realized he had referred to it as a 'kingdom.'

"Am I detecting a weakening of attitude on behalf of the Roman Catholic church?" asked Edgar with a look of surprise.

"I'm not against having a physical image of heaven. If heaven is a planet on the edge of the universe, then so be it. If people don't believe in an afterlife because there is no view of heaven, then I don't see any harm in knowing that heaven is a planet, if that's what it takes to get them believing. If Rapoe is God, and God is invisible, then I don't have a problem with that either."

"It sounds to me that Dr. Clay has another convert," said Edgar, walking away. John found himself sitting down, thinking about what he'd just said.

Chapter Eight.

Dr. Clay started the discussion saying, "Let me say from the outset, I am not an evangelist and never will be. I believe that Rapoe is God because of what I've seen and heard. I have also had the benefit of nearly two years in Rapoe's company, witnessing things you have yet to see. I hope that once this weekend is over, that some or all of you will be similarly enlightened. Would anybody like to comment?" he asked, scanning the faces for a response. John Mahoney raised his hand, saying,

"I feel naturally obligated to take the first crack at this one seeing I do represent the See of Rome. Before we resumed, I had been speaking with Edgar about this, and it occurred to me that I don't have a problem in thinking that God is invisible or that he lives on some massive planet hidden away in the corner of the universe. I told Edgar, as I'm saying to you, if that's what it takes to get people believing in God, then let it happen. I don't believe the Catholic Church will be a supporter of these theories any time soon." He paused briefly thinking of that possibility. "For me, this whole experience makes me re-analyze everything I've learned up to this point in my life. And that's a good thing. We always need to go back to the drawing-board whenever the opportunity arises. I don't believe that Rapoe is God, but I'm not against other people believing it. That's all I want to say at this juncture. I'm fascinated by everything that's happened so far. Thank you."

"Anyone else?" asked Dr. Clay.

"I want to believe that Rapoe is God," said a voice at the back, to which everybody turned and saw that it was General Blenfold, which not only surprised the audience, but nobody was more shocked than Dr. Clay who stared wide-eyed at the general who was seated in the corner of the hall. The general stood up and strolled up the center of the audience, saying, "I have been an observer to the events of the past 24 hours in much the same way as you. From a full-disclosure viewpoint, let me say that I have been privy to the nature of the program for quite some time, but not the content. I wasn't interested in the agenda as my mission was to ensure the group's full security and safe transport to and from this facility. However, it is impossible to ignore everything that has ensued, and I feel I must give my opinion on the proceedings thus far." He climbed the few steps to the small stage, turned to the audience and continued; "Dr. Clay has assembled an intriguing array of participants - all scholars and leaders in your respective fields. All my life, I have learned to plan for every eventuality, thankfully I got most things right. I've planned this mission in the same way as I've always done, but nothing would have prepared me for what I have seen and heard. I am not surprised by your skepticism nor your disbelief. I do want to say a few things. I have witnessed the painstaking work that Dr. Clay has put into this event this past year. I have no hesitation in saying that he is a dedicated professional who has staked his career on this weekend — the second thing I want to say concerns Rapoe. My officers represent the finest group of professionals one could wish for, all experts in their own right. They have gone to exhaustive measures to investigate all elements concerning our visitor and found nothing. As Dr. Clay has already indicated, Rapoe is not there! He is transmitting from somewhere out in space. Rapoe exists!" At that moment, the audience muttered amongst themselves, clearly surprised that a United States general was in full support of what Dr. Clay had said and done. The general continued, saying - "My final point is a personal one, and not as a doctrine of the United States government." The general scratched his eyebrow as he considered his thoughts, before looking up and saying, "I said I'd like to believe that Rapoe is God from many viewpoints, chief among them being that the world would finally have definite proof of His existence. Religion has always been at the forefront of most of the world's bloodshed. It would put an end to worldwide divisions amongst those who believe and those who never have. It should make the people of this planet stand united for the first time since our creation. I'm a military man, always have been. You are the world's experts in your respective fields, and you should address these matters you are witnessing with the utmost diligence on behalf of humanity. The other reason I give for wanting to believe Rapoe is God is purely a personal one. I'm not a God-fearing man, but I am God-aware. I have never gone along with the accepted stories of creation. To me, as a military man, it never made sense. However, I never had any evidence to make me want to change my viewpoint until now. I am seeing and hearing things that I've always wanted to see and hear. It's not nearly enough, as yet, but it's certainly a darned sight better than the stuff forced down our throats since we were born. That's it for now. Thank you," he said, returning to his seat beside Dr. Clay, who continued to stare at the general with a look of complete admiration.

"Thank you, General Blenfold for your input," said Dr. Clay standing up in front of the audience. "I hadn't thought about the consequences of admitting to the world that Rapoe is God, but you have put it into context quite vividly. As the general said, we all need to put aside our preconceived conceptions of everything we believe in, both scientifically and spiritually. If we believe that Rapoe is God, then it is up to us to disclose this information to the world, and above all, convince them as to why we do believe it to be so. That is not going to be an easy task. Even with our influences, people will always be skeptical and downright affronted in a lot of cases. That is why I invited our two celebrities, Lance and Zapper. They have a huge influence on an enormous amount of people through their fame and their social media outlets." He turned towards Lance and Zapper, saying - "Lance, Zapper, I am not putting either of you under any pressure to do anything. I invited you here to see for yourself. If, at the end of this weekend you find that you could join me in doing something, then and only then, will I ask for your assistance." Zapper and Lance shook their heads in acknowledgment. "Does anybody else have something to contribute?" asked Dr. Clay.

"We have learned very little about the sciences that go to prove what Rapoe is saying," said astronomer, Frank Dipple. "What about black holes? How does Rapoe configure that into the construction of the universe? Then there's our old friend 'gravity.' He hasn't once mentioned that. I would need the answers to these critical topics before I could even think about the spiritual side of things."

"I acknowledge what you're saying, Frank. If the audience agrees, I will ask Rapoe to address these concerns if that is the majority wish," added Dr. Clay. The muted response told him that most were happy for Rapoe to return. Dr. Clay put his fingers to his temples and almost immediately, Rapoe said,

"I have listened to your conversations, and I am pleased with what I've heard. I know you are all in earnest about doing what is right. I think it best at this stage to introduce you to someone who also had doubts about my kingdom and me. I told you earlier that I had come across one other planet that contained life comparable to yours. That planet, called Janza, is in a galaxy many light years away from your Milky Way galaxy. I came across it hundreds of millions of years before I discovered planet earth. The person who you are about to meet was even more skeptical than all of you when I first introduced myself to him. I will call upon him now to explain all of these things to you in a way that should make it easier for you to understand. His name is Mahh, and he is from the planet Janza." Everybody was stunned. Suddenly, everything was taking a new dimension. People looked at one another in shock, wondering what was about to unfold.

    Dr. Clay was as surprised as everybody. Rapoe had not disclosed that this would be happening. He sat down beside the general who was similarly transfixed. They all waited, wondering what was to happen.

Chapter Nine.

"I can't see," said John Mahoney, as he stood up holding his eyes.

"Help me, someone, please!" cried Mary-Rose, holding her hands to her face.

"Do not be afraid," were the words that everybody heard themselves speak. "You are about to see a vision of the planet Janza. This time you will hear the words of Mahh in your voices," added Rapoe.

"Try to breathe easily. Take long, deep breaths," said Dr. Clay, trying to get everybody to remain calm.

The darkness disappeared as they saw blurred images behind their opened eyes. It took a moment for everything to become apparent. Planets whisked by against a black background. Everybody looked around at the amazing sights of stars and planets that filled the vastness. It took some moments for everyone to catch their breaths. Suddenly, the darkness expanded as the stars disappeared from view. They all frowned wondering what was to happen next?

"Look, what's that?" asked Lila Thompson.

"It looks like three stars in alignment," said astronomer, Frank Dipple. "No, but wait. They're separating! The outermost stars seem to be drifting away from the central star," he added.

"That center star is not a star. Welcome to my planet, Janza," said their voices. "My name is Mahh, which is your people's pronunciation, not the way my people pronounce it. It feels strange to be speaking in this way, but Rapoe assures me that we can understand one another." He remained silent, allowing his audience to grasp the majesty of what they were seeing. It was spellbindingly beautiful. The planet Janza opened up in front of them. It was bathed in a bright blue haze and appeared to have two suns in the distance. As they got closer, they could see massive oceans with no visible land. The seas seemed to go on forever.

"Where are the people?" asked Zapper.

"All in good time," added Mahh. "I believe Janza is many times bigger than your planet. It must be hard for you to comprehend the magnitude of what you are seeing. We are a water planet energized by two stars.

Our world formed in much the same way as planet earth. We were fortunate to have the protection of our two mighty stars, allowing us to exist in relative obscurity within our galaxy. We have no landmass, only seas. Come with me now while I try to show you our world." People felt their throats dry up, and their hearts beat faster, not knowing what to expect. The more they traveled under the water, the more they calmed down. The silence offered no anxiety. It made them relax, making them want to listen to their breathing. Then Mahh said,

"Our world has an iron core, much greater than yours, which throws off a magnetic field that protects us from our sun's radiation. It is a planet bathed in constant sunlight. We create our darkness by submerging ourselves deep within our oceans, just like the creatures of your deep oceans on your earth. We have to be careful about our exposure to the sunlight as we could easily become over-exposed to radiation and die. We learned to live with our suns. We were fortunate to have such a sizeable planet that could cater for two huge stars. We know it will only be a matter of time before the stars engulf us." Mahh remained silent, knowing his audience were enthralled by what they were seeing. The colors were magnificent. The blues changed from azure to navy, then sapphire to turquoise all in an instant. There were hues of green that changed from lime to olive and back again to blue. The entire palette was stunning in its softness and tranquility. Then the sequence was suddenly destroyed, smashed into a contradiction by the sight of a creature so terrifying in its form that everybody leaned backward with fright. They wanted to tear the picture from their minds but found that they could not do that. Then the creature vanished, and the voice said,

"I must apologize for the intrusion of a Lafette. It is one of the friendlier creatures that inhabit our world. I believe it is about the same size as one of your elephants. As you can see, our creatures are enormous. Then again, you must understand our world is equally so, making the creatures proportionate to our size." Mahh went silent again as the images continued. There were turtle-like animals with enormous shells. There were eel-like fish and something like octopuses, but with many more tentacles. Massive shoals of fish gathered in balls and appeared to be feeding on something. The audience were frightened when their vision went black as if they had stopped receiving any communication. Then they heard their voices say, "What you will see presently is one of our greatest and most terrifying inhabitants." Their vision gradually cleared from darkness to light, as the impediment moved away to reveal a terrifying mammoth that defied all of their imaginations. "It is called a Dameneni," said Mahh. "It is a hundred times larger than your blue whale and spends its life foraging. We estimate its size at something like a half a mile long in your language. It is aggressive, but fortunately, it spends its time away from the deep where my people live." Everybody looked at the slowly disappearing suns as they traveled deeper. They remained enthralled by the number of sea creatures. It took a long time before darkness set in. Then Mahh spoke again, saying - "We float upwards towards the light every time we need to replenish the chemicals in our bodies. We don't have days as you do on earth. We do not need for time as we control how much daylight we require. We become invisible when we approach the light. It means the sunlight can penetrate our bodies very quickly, so we don't become too exposed. Secondly, and more importantly, it also means predators cannot see us. We came about by chance. The sea creatures were the original inhabitants on Janza, in much the same way as when the dinosaurs ruled your planet. We, like Rapoe, were born with a great intellect that allowed us to devise methods to protect ourselves. We were created at roughly the same time as you, around 4 billion years ago. I understand that your earth lived through troublesome periods. We were fortunate as our two suns repelled any asteroids or other planets that came close, much the same way as Jupiter continues to protect your planet." Suddenly everything went dark and remained that way for a few moments. It was Lance who was the first to say anything.

"What are those lights in the distance? There must be thousands of them."

"Many millions," answered Mahh.

"Oh my God, look at that!" said a startled Mary-Rose," staring open-mouthed at what her vision was showing her. "It's beautiful," she announced, as everybody became entranced by what they were seeing. The darkness was now full of color, as billions of glowing objects lit up the ocean.

"We can create our energy to make artificial light in much the same way as your deep-sea creatures do. We have perfected it to meet our requirements. Our luminosity is an early warning system as we have many enemies in the deep, but we have learned to live with them. These are my people," concluded Mahh, allowing his audience to take in the breathtaking beauty of what they were witnessing.

"It's like daylight," said Zapper. "It's amazing!"

"Stunning," said astronomer Laurence Shelvey. Then Mahh resumed, saying -

"In a moment you will see one of our great cities." The audience waited with bated breath wondering what was about to happen. Another five minutes passed before their wonderment turned to amazement. Massive pillars stood hundreds of feet high standing close to other pillars of various sizes. They were bathed in fluorescence and seemed to go on forever. Masses of small creatures flitted from one opening to another and seemed to be as curious about their visitors as their visitors were of them. "The buildings you see are made from the mineral deposits on the ocean beds. They are impenetrable and built many thousands of years ago. Our people inhabit about a quarter of the deep ocean bed. We feed on the multitude of minerals that bathe our seafloor. We do not have hydrothermal vents or tectonic plates like you do on your planet. While you look at the visions in front of you, I would like to explain certain things. We are inhabitants of the sea. We do not have a physical shape like you. We breathe oxygen just like you but in higher densities. We have all of the nutrients we require for our well being. We know the destructive forces that exist in the universe, and we also know it will only be a matter of time before we become a part of that destruction. Our two suns are destined to collide at some stage. When that happens, our world will disappear. The same thing will happen to you sometime in the future. A universe is an incredible place full of wonder. Just like you, we don't know the answers to many of the things that make our universe.

We've known about black holes, pulsars, and quasars, yet, we are none the wiser even though we have had the benefit of knowing of their existence for millions of years before you. Rapoe knows these answers, but He has said we wouldn't understand until we became one with him. As a people, we never had any illusions about where we came from or about our destiny. Our creation was the result of the composition of elements. We had no single Creator and never needed the adornment of idols. We have long lifespans; some of our people have lived for thousands of years. We don't get sick with diseases or deformities. We don't kill each other, and we don't have crime. We are a loving people. Rapoe offered us eternal life in return for our love and belief. He was someone who promised us happiness beyond our expectations. At first, there was only a handful of us who were happy to believe in Rapoe. Just like humans, we too needed a sign. We were impressed by his intelligence which was far superior to ours. We called on him for assistance when we came under attack by a Dameneni. We had no defenses against such a beast that could swallow many millions of us in seconds. One day, the Damenini disappeared never to return to our depth. Rapoe promised us that we would never again come to any harm from such a creature. His promise has held ever since. When we did decide to believe in Him, our whole lives changed for the better. We had found someone who gave us unconditional love and who promised us eternal life. Perhaps it was easier for us to believe in Him because we understood that He wasn't some mythical figure that came out of nowhere. We knew he had an amazing intellect. He had a home - a planet. We didn't have to invent stories that made Him out to be someone or something that he wasn't! He is now showing you these truths about Himself. There should be no more doubts. Once we started that belief, we never turned away from it. When a person shows you, such love, how can you not believe in that person? It was His offer of eternal life that convinced my people that we should join with Him, knowing that the love we had for one another would live on for eternity. You have taken thousands of years to get to this point in your history. You have had many obstacles along the way, chief among them being humanity itself. Rapoe has shown me your history and a lot of it I have found hard to comprehend. You have a beautiful world, yet you go out of your way to destroy it! You have love and intelligence in abundance, yet you don't use these gifts wisely. You don't show love for one another in the same way as us. We would never have allowed such traits to enter our world. I understand that Rapoe has shown you that same love, yet you refuse it. How can you do this, when he gave you the great gift of His only son, whom you killed!" A long silence prevailed. Most of the audience thought deeply about what they had heard. Dr. Clay allowed the silence to continue until theologian, Peter Shapely, raised his hand, asking,

"What would you advise us to do if you were us?" Mahh responded, saying,

"You should ask yourselves what is wrong with someone offering you eternal life and who asks for only love and belief in return? You should grasp it, as we have done. Why would you live your lives knowing only death as your reward? How can you accept death over the promise of eternal life or at least the hope of one? Humanity has not evolved. You are still a single race, not a complex one. Stop looking out, and start looking in.

You have untapped resources within yourselves. It's time to look for them. You must find your soul!" An eerie quiet enveloped everybody as they continued to look at the beautiful images in front of them. Nobody could find the words to interrupt such a spectacle, and they all wanted it to go on forever. Dr. Clay looked at his guests and saw that even the scientists, were deep in thought. He waited for a considerable time to elapse before saying,

"I think that's a good juncture in which to take some time out. What Mahh has shown us has been spectacular. What he has said has been no less fascinating and thought-provoking." Dr. Clay looked at his watch, saying, "It's coming up to 8 pm on a Saturday following an eventful and controversial 24 hours. I would suggest that we should refresh ourselves and get ready for dinner. We should use that opportunity to discuss everything we've witnessed. Rapoe and I have agreed to meet up again in the morning after we've all rested. Let us regroup in an hour or so. Thank you." Dr. Clay moved behind the curtained area accompanied by the general.

"Were you expecting to witness what just happened?" asked the general. Dr. Clay finished drinking from his water bottle, saying,

"I was as surprised as everybody else, general. Rapoe never ceases to amaze. During the past year, he told me that he would have some surprises in store, but I'd never have guessed about a visit to another planet. What did you think of Mahh and the planet Janza?" The general, in his usual manner, didn't need time to consider his response.

"There was no trickery involved. My team monitored everything and didn't discover any influences from any satellites. What we saw was genuine. The thing that bothers me is," continued the general, stopping mid-sentence before saying, "how did Rapoe manage to get rid of the problem of the behemoth called the Dameneni? After all, it was this act that convinced the inhabitants of Janza to believe in Him, and you cannot control a creature of that size without a visit!" Dr. Clay continued to look at the general as he considered his words. He hadn't thought about the logistics of solving the problem of the Dameneni.

"That's a good point, general. Perhaps it lends credence to Rapoe's statement of having parted the Red Sea!" he suggested. The general nodded and shrugged, as the two of them made their way back to their quarters.

Chapter Ten.

Most people stood around with drinks in hand talking to each other, now that they had freshened up and changed their clothes. The officers had created a room-like area by blocking off a section of the hall. They were making their final preparations for dinner and had created a large dining table with enough chairs around it for all of the guests.

"Astounding," said Fred Pinkton to those around him. "I was instrumental in developing the ISS. At that time, we thought it was something amazing to be able to do what we'd done; now, I've just been given a tour of the universe without leaving my seat! We have visited an inhabited planet! Astounding!" he repeated.

"I'm afraid I'm also confused, but for many different reasons," added John Mahoney overhearing what he'd said. "If I accept what I've seen and heard, then everything I have learned so far is worthless. It means that humanity has been under several illusions about their existence! The paradox is that my church has effectively been preaching heresy! Who will believe me, even though I've seen it with my own eyes?" he concluded with a dazed look.

"So where do we go from here?" asked Lance, looking at Zapper and Andrew. They had been wondering that very same thing. It was Andrew who said,

"Like everybody else I've spoken to, I cannot explain anything I've seen, but I will say this," he said, nodding towards the area outside the building - "That is real! I can say that for certain. None of what we've seen and heard is human-made. The way we were able to hear our voices, and then the knock-out punch of Janza!" He shook his head slowly from side to side as he continued to look out the window towards the sky.

"I don't see how you couldn't believe the stuff that's happened," followed Zapper. "You'd want to be stupid not to believe it, especially when it's happened right before your very eyes." Mary-Rose stood alone near the bar area and appeared to be in a type of trance. Peter Shapely approached her, saying,

"Are you looking forward to dinner? The officers seem to have put in a lot of effort." She turned and smiled, saying,

"I don't think I'll be able to eat anything, but I thank you for joining me. You're a theologian, Mr. Shapely. You must have lots of thoughts running through your head - good, clever thoughts. I'd value your opinion on what you think that's happening?" Peter took a sip of wine, smacked his lips together and smiled, saying,

"I may be a theologian, Mary-Rose, but nothing, and I mean nothing, could have prepared me for what I've witnessed these past 24 hours. Don't think you're the only one that's in shock. I'm as bad as everybody else. I'm meant to be an expert in the supernatural, but what I've seen goes way beyond that boundary. I've been fascinated by the scientist's reactions, who all seem to be baffled, especially having visited Janza and heard what Mahh had to say. I've remained aloof regarding my opinions thus far. I know that I'm probably going to be confronted by Dr. Clay and have to account for myself. I'm not at all sure that I'm ready to do so. Here, cheers, perhaps after a few of these I might have a eureka moment,' he said tinkling Mary-Rose's wineglass and gulping down his drink.

"If any of this is true, then the science world is going to flip," said Fred Pinkton, addressing his small group.

"I'm impressed at the scientific honesty of both Rapoe and Mahh," said astronomer, Frank Dipple. "Let me explain. If this were some computer-generated artificial nonsense, then the two protagonists would surely claim to rule the world or say things that would scare us. But, they haven't done that. They could have pretended that they knew the answers to the black-hole phenomenon. Instead, Mahh said he didn't know, even though they've had the benefit of discovering these phenomena long before we did."

"But Mahh did say that Rapoe knows the answers to those questions," interrupted his colleague, Laurence Shelvey.

"I agree, Laurence, but they have also been forthright about who they are, and in Mahh's case, he told us straight that he didn't believe in Rapoe at first and that it took his people many thousands of years to come around. They have both confirmed what we were beginning to think back here on earth - that there are billions, more than likely trillions of planets in the universe but precious few that contain intelligent life in a form that we can all understand and deal with."

"They also concur about the inevitable destruction of all planets at some stage," added Laurence.

"I know that Laurence, but Rapoe is not proclaiming to be some mystical figure, as we were led to believe through the centuries; instead, he's offering us a way out, and a logical one at that."

"Yes, but with eternal life!" added Fred Pinkton, who had been listening to the conversation. "Come on; you cannot seriously contemplate that there is such a thing?" There was a general silence until Andrew said,

"What about Mahh? He said his people had a natural lifespan of thousands of years. If that's the case, then an eternal life offered by Rapoe may not seem out of the question, especially when he had demonstrated that he was here when our world was developing; when dinosaurs ruled and when man first came into existence. From what I've heard, I wouldn't doubt that what he says isn't too far from the truth."

"That's quite different to your earlier views," butted in Lila Thompson. I seem to remember you throwing buckets of iced water on this whole charade less than twenty-fours ago. I believe you mentioned that the entire affair was scandalous." Andrew was embarrassed. He pursed his lips, looked Lila straight in the face, saying,

"You're quite right, Lila. I did say that it was scandalous, but I'm also willing to admit when my views have changed. I believe that what we've all seen is factual. I do not doubt that. There is nothing contrived about any of this. What is in contention are our views as to whether anything we've heard is right or wrong. We have no justification for accepting either possibility. That's where the debate has to start."

"I appreciate your honesty, and I hope my remarks didn't offend you?" added Lila.

"Not in the slightest. I'm glad of the opportunity to clarify my position."

"The inhabitants of Janza are tiny fish-like creatures. How can they have that much intelligence?" asked Frank Dipple shaking his head from side to side.

"Size doesn't matter when it comes to intelligence. We only have to look at our own three and a half pounds of mush that makes up our brain to understand it. Consider Dr. Stephen Hawking and the restrictions imposed upon his body, yet he housed one of the greatest scientific minds this world has ever known," added Fred Pinkton.

"I don't think you have to wonder very hard about their capabilities when you consider how they were able to accomplish their engineering marvels. One look at any of their structures will tell you that," added Lila Thompson.

The general discussions continued for another short while until Dr. Clay announced that dinner was ready and asked people to take their seats.

Chapter Eleven.

People sat together in much the same order as they had done since they arrived. Zapper, Lance, and Andrew sat left-side of Dr. Clay, while Peter and Mary-Rose joined Fred Pinkton. John Mahoney, Lila, and Edgar Snipes, moved alongside the two astronomers, Frank Dipple, and Laurence Shelvey. The general whispered something to Dr. Clay before leaving the group to their discussion. Dr. Clay stood up and addressed everybody, saying -

"Please enjoy your meal. You should find something to whet your appetite. Talk amongst yourselves while you enjoy your food, then after we've finished eating we should discuss everything that has arisen." Dr. Clay nodded to the officers who started to serve the food. Another officer offered wine and soft drinks. Dr. Clay generally chatted with those around him as he too enjoyed his meal. When most people had finished their main course, Dr. Clay stood and cleared his throat, saying -

"It has pleased me greatly that all of you have remained. I hope that by now you'll understand the anxieties I felt before inviting you all here. None of what you've seen has been contrived. I have not forced anything upon you, bearing in mind that the other invitees have departed willingly." Dr. Clay paused for a moment, giving some thought to his next question. He had wondered whether it was appropriate but decided that it was time for everybody to step up to the plate. "Could I ask for a show of hands-on whether you now believe that Rapoe is God?" A sudden silence permeated the room as one person looked at another, wondering if they were about to commit themselves. Mary-Rose put her hand up immediately. Dr. Clay was surprised and delighted to see Zapper raise his hand, and just as he was about to start the general discussion, Edgar Snipes raised his hand to everybody's shock and surprise. There were audible gasps from just about everybody.

"Zapper, Edgar, I admire your honesty, and I'm sure everybody would be interested to hear the reasons for your change of mind," asked Dr. Clay.

Zapper looked at Edgar, who prompted him to be his guest.

"I've said before that I'm no scientist, but I'm a believer in many things, especially people. A lot of people have been good to me throughout my life, and I've learned to be streetwise. I think that's what comes across in my music. Dr. Clay, what I've seen and heard here on this island leaves me in no doubt that Mr. Rapoe is God, or at least somebody exceptional that has amazing powers. I can't understand why the scientists can't believe what they've seen with their own eyes. I was raised as a Baptist and seeing what I've seen makes me think how it must have felt when Jesus performed all those miracles in front of people, and still, they didn't believe in him! You told us at the start to open our hearts and our minds, well I'd also add to open our eyes and ears. I can't wait to hear what Rapoe wants us to do? That's all I'm sayin'."

"Thank you, Zapper. That was very enlightening and heartfelt," said Dr. Clay turning towards Edgar Snipes. "Edgar, as one of the world's best-known philanthropists, I think everybody is keen to know what happened to convince you that Rapoe is God?" Edgar smiled and sat back in his seat, looking comfortable and assured as he said,

"If some technological genius has contrived this whole affair, then I salute everybody involved. However, I know that this is not the case as there are too many experts attending not so easily fooled. Also, I've known Dr. Clay for many years, and he is not the type of man to waste anybody's time. So, that takes me to the comings and goings of this amazing weekend. I don't believe that I've ever asked myself so many questions about the origins of life before coming on this trip. The admittance by Rapoe that He did not create the earth rests easily with me. I have never been an advocate of such a dogma laid down by so-called experts, particularly the church. I, like everybody else, have been browbeaten since I was a child by parents and teachers who meant well, but who themselves were also subject to wayward teachings. As others within our group have pointed out, science has very recently confirmed the viewpoint that circumstances beyond anybody's control indeed created us. Then Rapoe floored us all when he announced that he hadn't created man, but had found us! That, for me, was the knockout blow. Again, it cleared a lot of doubt that had been consigned to a dormant part of my brain many years ago, and I had assumed that I would never have needed to resurrect such thoughts. I could never rectify our creation to some unknown and unseen being. I had a normal faith that had been increasingly subject to debate, and faith was the continual loser. Science is once again providing evidence that we have evolved from a series of amazing incidences and coincidences that support Rapoe's statements. Which brings me to the most recent revelations in the shape of Mahh and his home called Janza. I was in awe, as I'm sure everybody was at what we saw. Here we had someone speak to us from another planet, something that none of us thought would ever be possible in our lifetimes. Mahh explained succinctly how his inhabitants learned to believe in Rapoe because of what was on offer. I also like the fact that neither Rapoe or Mahh are forcing anybody to believe in them. They have stated the facts about their existence and Rapoe has explained how he came across us and our planet. To me, it's all very logical, and I'm a fervent believer in logic. All of this leads me to believe in Rapoe and what he has to say," said Edgar, sipping his replenished wine. Dr. Clay sighed deeply with relief and contentment, knowing that the revered Edgar Snipes was committed to the believers.

"Thank you, Edgar, for your analysis and your honesty. I believe that everybody here would have a hard time trying to debate anything you've said. Everybody will have more than enough opportunity to express their views and opinions. Let me give my take on what Edgar and Zapper have said as it relates to me. When I said that I believed that Rapoe was God, I wasn't entirely honest. I was believing in Him because I'm a scientist. I wasn't privy to knowing anything about Janza or Mahh until I saw it at the same time as all of you. I hadn't thought of the spiritual aspect of any of it. I didn't need to, because simply finding out all the answers to a lifetime of scientific questions would be the culmination of everything I stand for. I would no longer have to guess because Rapoe could tell me everything! But, I now realize that this is something much bigger than all of that.

We have been privileged to learn the truth. Let's examine what we have learned. We know that there was never a Creator, something that science and scientists have been expounding for over a hundred years. One up for science. We have had it confirmed by beings far superior to us in every way that we are unable to transport ourselves around the universe; that there is no magical energy available that would allow us to do that in a reasonable timescale and still be safe. Mahh has shown us how his peoples lived peacefully and prospered, while we here on earth continually cause ourselves harm. Should we care whether or not the God that people believed in was someone divine, someone 'out there'? Isn't it far better to have proof that the 'out there' is another being on another planet, somewhere in the universe? Isn't it enriching and powerfully satisfying to know that that being, that new God, is someone who loves us? Someone who has perfect intellect? Someone who wants us? I don't know about the rest of you, but that is someone I want and not for any scientific reason." Dr. Clay allowed his words to sink in before saying, "I have wrestled with these thoughts for well over a year. I have had a lot more time to think about it than any of you. We are in no hurry to come to any conclusions. It's taken humanity many thousands of years to get to where we are now. Who would like to say something?" Everybody was in deep thought. It was Peter Shapely who first spoke, saying,

"As a theologian, this trip has thrown my very being into turmoil. I never imagined that I would witness something like this in my lifetime. We are all in a unique situation surrounded by the world's experts in their field of science. That gives me solace. Firstly, I know that what I'm experiencing is not something I'm doing alone. I can look around me and know that all of you are suffering in your thoughts, just like me." Peter shook his head from side to side, saying - "I'm not a liberal theologian, but at the same time I'm not too conventional either. I have now been shocked into submission by what I've seen and heard. By shocked, I mean that I cannot refute any of it. I have to say what I've seen, and that means I am forced to believe, yet all my doctrines tell me to deny it. These are the things that concern me. Zapper asked the question of how could we not believe what our eyes see? As a witness to all of these things, and a supposed expert in my field, I should not have any difficulty in agreeing with Zapper, but to do so would mean throwing everything I've been conditioned to believe, out the window. It's as if I've wasted my entire life believing in something wrong!" Peter leaned his elbows on the table and rubbed his face with both hands. He waited for a long moment, sighed deeply, and said - "I have to believe what I'm seeing. I have to believe that Rapoe is God!" There was an immediate outburst of talk amongst the rest of the people.

"Peter, you're a theologian," said John. "You cannot change everything you've learned over your lifetime in 24 hours! You must detract what you've said."

"I believe that a person called Saul also had a similar epiphany on a certain road to Damascus, and he wasn't privy to what we're witnessing," said Lila looking at John.

"That's not the point, Lila. I'm talking about educated people reversing a lifetime's study and belief," added John.

"I hear what you're saying, John," interjected Peter. "I'm a theologian, just like you and Lila.

I'm just saying that the evidence is quite compelling and that I'm entitled to my changing beliefs. Look at the New testament. Look how the apostles came to believe!"

"Yes, and there were twelve of them also," added Fred Pinkton, looking around at the faces." Dr. Clay remained quiet, allowing everybody to consider their thoughts and their words. It was Frank Dipple who spoke next.

"Look, I'm an astronomer, and like most scientists, I always ignore the God question. In my 35 years, I have never heard the God question arising amongst my peers. However, I have to admit that the things I've witnessed on this island make me rethink my position. As someone has said already, the evidence is compelling. God believers never had any foundation for their beliefs other than the people who wrote the gospels, two of whom were witnesses to those events. I don't doubt that if humanity had witnessed even half of what we've seen, then the whole world would have no excuse for not believing." Frank rose from his seat and stretched his legs, considering his next words. "So far, this conversation has been between the theological side with no input from the scientific side. As someone said previously, it's like trying to mix oil and water. The science community has always battled with the religious ones, and vice versa. So here's something from left field." He turned to the group and paused for a moment before saying, "I believe Rapoe is your God!" Everybody gasped.

"You can't be serious, Frank?" said astronomer Laurence Shelvey. Frank held up his hand, saying,

"I have never been more serious, Laurence. Note I said 'your God' - Rapoe is not my God. I am saying that all the evidence thus far points to a supernatural being that offers humanity eternal life. Based on the evidence, I have no reason to doubt any of it. I'm not saying I'm a believer. I am saying that this 'God' is the genuine article," he concluded and sat back down.

"I thank you for your honesty," said Mary-Rose, which made everybody turn in her direction.

"Go ahead, Mary-Rose. Feel free to say anything you want as you are as important as anybody else in this group," added Dr. Clay. Mary-Rose stood up and looked at Frank saying,

"I respect Mr. Dipple for what he said. It must have been tough for him to stand up in front of his kind and say what he did. At the same time, he said he's not a believer, but he respected those that have changed their minds because of what they've seen and heard. I was brought up to be a believer, and I've carried that belief all through my life. I never questioned any of it because to do so would be a mortal sin." She smirked as she said those words. "I suppose my religious beliefs were always based around the bible and nurtured by fear. This weekend has taught me differently. Rapoe has said he never wanted people to believe in him out of fear. Now that I think about it, I feel a lot happier inside because of those words. We all know the difference between right and wrong, so why would we need a set of commandments and church rules to keep us onside? If I'm being asked to choose between the God I thought I knew and the God that is Rapoe, then I choose Rapoe. I want to go about my life loving a God without any fear, and when I sin, I'll make my confession from the heart and strive not to sin again," she said blushing, before adding, "Thank you for listening," Her words resonated with the group because of Mary-Rose's honesty. They could see she was in earnest about what she had said. Dr. Clay decided it was time for him to contribute. He stood up, saying,

"Thank you Mary-Rose and everybody for contributing to the discussion. We need to take time out to consider everything. I would suggest we should take time out alone. Go for a walk around the island. Treat your time as a retreat of sorts. Ask yourselves the questions that need asking, but by all means, be truthful with yourselves. It's approaching 10 pm. Tomorrow, Sunday is our last day together, and it promises to be as enlightening as everything else we have seen and heard. Please try and get a good night's sleep. I would suggest that following breakfast we should all gather together outside at around 8.30 am. Until then, I wish you all pleasant dreams." Dr. Clay shook everybody's hands and asked Edgar if he could have one of his tablets?

"Certainly, Dr. Clay," he said, taking the pillbox from his jacket.

"I feel I'll need something to keep me alert for tomorrow," explained, Dr. Clay, putting the pill in his pocket before departing for his quarters. As he walked, he turned back to take a look at the people and wondered how they were going to feel after tomorrow's event, knowing that Sunday would bring the most significant shock of all.

Chapter Twelve.

Dr. Clay lay on his bed, unable to sleep, as he pondered what was to happen later. He checked the time which told him it was approaching 5 am. and decided to take Edgar's pill in the hope that it kept him alert throughout the day. He made his way to the bathroom to freshen up and have a shower. There was no point in prolonging the agony of not being able to sleep.

A half-hour later, he opened the door to the early rising sun and saw that the three scientists were under the vapor looking up.

"Good morning Fred, Frank, Laurence. I trust you didn't have a good night's sleep," he said, smiling.

"None of us shut an eye, Dr. Clay," added Frank. "We were trying to figure out Rapoe's means of transport with no success." They all looked upwards as Dr. Clay said,

"As I said before, Rapoe uses the vapor purely as a means of focus. We had to look at something and seeing that Rapoe is invisible and not here, I suppose it was the only way to make any sense out of what he was trying to do."

"Why did Rapoe pick on you to deliver his message," asked Fred. Dr. Clay shrugged, saying,

"Beats me, Fred. I've asked myself that question a hundred times. I'm not an ideal candidate when it comes to dealing with the spiritual. I'm the complete antithesis of belief of any kind apart from the scientific one. I must admit that since it happened, I have studied the bible in great detail, especially the New Testament. All of the twelve apostles needed to be convinced before they tagged along. Saul, or Paul, as he became, was probably the most intellectual of them all. He was also a tyrant in one respect, having tormented the christians of the day, and the one who condemned Stephen, the first martyr. Paul became the voice of God, traveling to all corners of the known civilized world, preaching the word, a belief that culminated in his horrible death. All of the apostles suffered a similar faith, including Matthew, who was a wealthy man in his own right, yet still, he became a believer and gave up everything. The bible is full of such accounts that have to make one sit up and take notice. These men became the ultimate ambassadors for the christian faith. Rapoe probably chose me because times have changed a great deal since those days. The apostles of that time wouldn't stand a chance of convincing people nowadays the way they did back then. Rapoe knows he needs a very different method for getting his message across. I guess I'm it."

"It can't be easy for you, having to convince others, especially knowledgeable people like us? Why didn't he pick the Pope or the President?" asked Laurence.

"Probably because they would be too hard to convince? Both of them are authoritarian in their way and not ideal candidates. I am not answerable to anybody, yet I have the belief of the world through my work. People would believe in me before they'd believe the President of the United States. Don't you think?" The three men shook their heads thoughtfully and agreed in silence. "To be honest with you, I would have much preferred not to have been anybody's candidate. I was quite happy doing my thing oblivious to any spirituality entering my closeted life. But, once Rapoe convinced me of everything, then I had to make a go of it. Hopefully, I haven't let him down." Dr. Clay looked around and noticed somebody in the distance. "Looks like there's another body that couldn't sleep," he said, pointing to a distant figure walking amongst the sands.

"That's Mary-Rose. I saw her heading that direction about an hour ago," said Frank.

"I think I'll go over to her and check that she's okay," said Dr. Clay, moving off in her direction. As he walked away, Laurence commented,

"I don't envy him his task. I wouldn't be able to do it, that's for sure." Fred and Frank nodded their agreement. Dr. Clay approached Mary-Rose from behind and coughed slightly so as not to alarm her. She was seated on the sand looking out to sea, and turned quickly and smiled, relieved to see Dr. Clay.

"Could you not sleep, Mary-Rose?"

"I'm afraid not — my minds all a jumble. I'm excited beyond belief," said Mary-Rose, as Dr. Clay sat down beside her.

"It's a beautiful island, but very isolated. I'd love to have a house here," he said, keeping the conversation light. He could see that Mary-Rose was in deep thought and waited for her to speak. She scribbled her index finger in the sand, saying,

"I was thinking of my mother before you arrived. I was wondering what she would make of all this? Then I thought that it's probably just as well that she's no longer with us, as she's more than likely with Rapoe in heaven as we speak. She never needed any proof of his existence. She had a blind faith like so many people. Had I not witnessed these things, I would probably have strayed from my beliefs eventually." Dr. Clay waited for Mary-Rose to finish before adding,

"Everybody needs some belief, even if it's not to believe. I remember when I first saw the famous 'Earthrise' photograph, taken by William Anders on Apollo 8 back in 1968. I was 12 years old when I saw it and I, like everybody else, marveled at the picture of earth's fragility. This beautiful blue orb suspended against a blackness sent a chill through my young body. It is a chill that remains with me to this day. That photograph hangs over my desk in my study, and any time I feel lost, I stare at this picture, and I don't feel alone; that picture enthuses me. That's the same feeling that I have right now, only a thousand times stronger. Knowing that Rapoe is out there, waiting for me - waiting for all of us - to give us an eternal life of love is beyond comprehension, yet deeply satisfying. That, above all else, encourages me and makes me want to make a success of it. I want to scream at the world and tell them to forget about the past. To throw away all of their agendas and get on with the business of living and loving one another." Mary-Rose sat wide-eyed, looking at Dr. Clay.

"Wow, Dr. Clay, that's so wonderful to hear you say something like that. I feel the same way, but am afraid to say it. I wish I had your strength." Dr. Clay smiled and looked out to sea, saying,

"Maybe we can all feed off one another. God knows we're going to need all of the support we can muster. But, tell me, Mary-Rose, what are you going to do back on the mainland? I presume Mr. Kingston won't be welcoming you back anytime soon?" Mary-Rose sighed, saying,

"No. That part of my career is over. That's for sure."

"What exactly were your duties?"

"I was known as his nurse, but I was a general girl-Friday. I was his secretary and human-resources manager, as well as everything else he wanted doing."

"So you're good with technology?"

"Not a problem. I can do most things."

"Then, when we get back, you can come and work with me, if that's something that would interest you?" Mary-Rose smiled broadly, saying,

"I'd love nothing more."

"Great, because after this weekend's events, we are going to be super busy and I'm going to need all the professional help I can muster," he said, shaking her hand enthusiastically.

*　　　*　　　*　　　*

"Oh man, I slept like a baby," announced Zapper sitting down at the table beside Lance, who was also eating his breakfast.

"I'm glad someone did because I never shut an eye. Did you take something?" he said nudging Zapper on the arm.

"No man, it's the first time I've slept without an upper or a downer. I have a ton of stuff in my bag, and I swear to God, or Rapoe, that I never touched a pill," said Zapper, happily munching some fruit and pancakes. "My biggest concern is what the hell I'm going to say to the people who are wondering where I'm at?" he said, swallowing a slice of pancake.

"What do you mean? Surely you told everyone that you were at this convention?" asked Lance.

"Are you kiddin"? Do you think that anyone would believe that Zapper Zee is at some science convention? No way, Jose. I told them all that I was digging out with some friends in Hawaii."

"At least you got part of the location right, after all, it is the Pacific," smiled Lance. "I'm worried that my wife has been calling me and getting no answer. I never told her that I would be incommunicado. Guess I'll have to ride that storm out when I get back."

"After she hears what you've been doin', I don't think you're gonna get any questions, because you'll be getting' your ass kicked into some loony bin. You know what I'm sayin'?" said Zapper finishing off his eggs. Lance chewed his food, thinking about what Zapper had said.

"On that point, what the hell are we supposed to do with everything we've learned? You're right; we could be all locked up when we try to explain that we spent the weekend having a pow-wow with God, oh, and by the way, he never made us or the world!" Zapper stopped eating and swallowed whatever food remained in his mouth. Then he said,

"I think that it's best to leave all of the explanations for the good doctor. I'm sayin' nothing," he affirmed, letting out a belch.

*   *   *   *

"We haven't spoken in any great depth about this weekend's events, Peter," said Lila. Peter drank his coffee, then said,

"I know, Lila. As two of the world's leading theologians, I suppose it is beholding upon us to trash this out as best we can."

"At least you've raised your flag in the believer's column, which I have to say, surprised me no end. Are you that convinced about the accuracy and authenticity of everything you've seen and heard?" she asked. Peter positively looked at her, saying,

"I have no doubt whatsoever, Lila. I'm also happy to amend all of the doctrines I've studied. I am forthright in my understanding. I'll stand up to anyone when I get back and support Dr. Clay with whatever he wants from me." Lila looked towards the window of the building and could discern the vapor hanging in midair. She thought about what she was about to say, adding,

"I cannot be that definite. Certainly, a strong case has been made by Dr. Clay this weekend, supported by Rapoe, Mahh, and what we saw on Janza. However, I cannot throw away a lifetime of learning based on one weekend. I need more time - more proof." Peter chuckled, saying,

"More proof, Lila! How could you possibly want more proof when you've seen so much! God himself has explained everything to you; about where He came from, where we came from and how He found us. We've heard from the leader of another planet and saw his amazing world. We heard how his people came to believe in Rapoe. Then, to cap it all, God tells us He wants us, and He promises us eternal life. Come on, Lila, what more could you possibly need to confirm what you already know?"

"I can't make my mind up that fast," she growled. "That's all I can say," said Lila storming off, leaving a confused Peter in her wake.

*   *   *   *

"How are you feeling, John," asked Andrew, sitting down next to him. "I see you haven't touched your breakfast. You should eat something." John held his head down, looking at his plate, and said nothing.

Andrew could see that John was miles away in thought. He decided to break the silence by saying,

"I couldn't sleep either. As an astrophysicist, I'm as bewildered as you with everything that's gone on. I want to be as positive as Dr. Clay, but I can't get my head around any of it. How about you?' John shook himself away from his thoughts and digested Andrew's question before replying,

"Befuddled is probably a good word to describe my brain. I'm not looking forward to getting back to Rome and trying to write a report on my visit. If I lie, then I'm a hypocrite to my ordained status. I think I'll stay here on this deserted island and wait for the end to come." Andrew chuckled, saying,

"Come on. It's not as bad as all that. It's been a revelation! It's not every day you get to talk to God in the flesh, or maybe not the flesh! We're in the same boat, you and I. I'm also considering denying everything I've witnessed and go about my life trying to forget that this weekend occurred. We both know we can't do that. I believe the best we can do is wait and see what Dr. Clay is going to advise and take it from there.

Nothing is going to happen overnight. Indeed, I'd say we'll mull over this for weeks, and more than likely have further meetings to get a general viewpoint on the way to progress matters."

"I can't wait that long. Too much has happened for me to ignore it and hope that it all disappears. Rapoe is there!" he said, pointing towards the window to the vapor. We heard him use his words in our voices! We visited a planet and heard from its leader that they believe in Him. How can I ignore all of that?"

"Then, don't ignore it. Remember, the apostles had much more difficult choices to make. They had no support infrastructure, yet they had to go out and try to convince the world to believe in God based on what they had seen and heard. You, on the other hand, have the support of some of the greatest minds on our planet."

"Would I have your support?" asked John looking at Andrew square in the face. Andrew turned towards the sky outside, thought for a moment, then turned to John saying,

"Unequivocally, yes. I would support you."

* * * *

Most people had finished their breakfast and waited around outside, looking up at the vapor. Dr. Clay stood talking with the general on the small podium when suddenly he put his hands to his temples, and everybody knew that signaled an event. They all gathered around and watched as he muttered something to the general and turned towards the group, saying,

"Okay, everybody, we're ready to proceed. There's a slight change to the way the communication will unfold. Instead of hearing the words using your voices, you will hear them from a different voice, but in the same manner as before. Please don't be alarmed. I hope by now that everybody is used to this arrangement." Dr. Clay waited until everybody was seated. He then turned towards the vapor and kept his fingers on his temple as he waited for a signal. Everybody looked around expectantly and wondered what new surprises awaited them. It took about a minute or so before the light shone through the haze. It appeared brighter this time, and then they heard the words,

"My name is Aneesh. You know me as Jesus!"

Chapter Thirteen.

Mary-Rose fainted immediately.

"Make way," said the general, moving quickly towards the prostrate Mary-Rose. He turned her on her side and held her head in his arms. Someone handed him some water, and once she swallowed a little, she began to revive. Others looked at one another, trying to understand what they'd heard.

"He said he was Jesus, right? inquired Lance.

"He said, Aneesh, and that we knew Him as Jesus," added Andrew.

"This is bizarre," added Lila, turning towards Dr. Clay, who remained calm, but concerned about the welfare of Mary-Rose. They managed to get her seated, and after a few moments, she got color back into her face.

"Are you okay, Mary-Rose?" asked Peter. She nodded, saying,

"I'm sorry for causing such a fuss. I got such a fright when I heard the voice say He was Jesus.

Did I imagine it?" The group looked towards Dr. Clay who said,

"Ladies and gentlemen, everybody should be seated." The group moved tentatively towards their seats and remained quiet waiting to hear the new voice. Peter held Mary-Rose's hand as Dr. Clay said,

"Please, Aneesh. Speak freely."

"I am speaking to you in the voice I used when I was on your earth; the same voice heard by Peter and all of the apostles. You have heard from my Father and seen the planet Janza and how those people came to believe in my Father's kingdom. Listen, while I try to explain. When my Father found your planet and your people, He knew it would be impossible to appear to the inhabitants as souls. They would never understand what they could not see. At the same time, we needed to announce ourselves discreetly if we were to have any hope of redeeming souls. It was my suggestion to be born as one of you. For that purpose, we chose a woman who could bear my spirit without human contamination. We also chose a poor family. In that way, we could blend into your humanity without any difficulty. Mary and

Joseph were a perfect family and are with us in our kingdom. I had a childhood like other children. The people were very primitive, and it took me many years to adapt to their ways, as my intelligence exceeded my physicality. I felt I had to be as one with you so that humanity could be as one with me. I spent my early years learning everything about your people and your world. I enjoyed the scriptures written about my Father. The early prophets were aware of my coming as told to them by my Father. I worked with Joseph, helping him as any son would do. I played with my half-brothers and sisters. I studied the writings of the Greeks and the Romans. When I felt I was ready, I set about my teaching. I performed my first miracles at Cana and recruited Simon Peter and his brother Andrew as my first disciples. Most of the disciples were known to me, and they followed me without hesitation. When I reported this to my Father, he was pleased. The actions of Peter and the other disciples encouraged us to continue with our work. The writings of the Gospels are correct. I had asked Peter not to describe me because my physical shape or description would not follow me into my Father's kingdom. I wanted the people to remember me for my works and my words, not for my appearance. I explained to my friends only what I thought they could understand. They had many questions, only some of which I could answer. I had said to them that if they didn't understand the earthy things I told them, then how could they expect to understand heavenly things? They were not like the people of today who know so much more. I couldn't tell them that my Father was on another planet and that it was His kingdom! Our only aim was to educate humanity to have a love for one another. The men who wrote the account of my life on earth did so with truth and understanding. The miracles I performed did not cause me any concern. I was happy to do them knowing that people might believe. I have said that unless the people witnessed my works, that they would never believe. At times it was frustrating, and I understood why people got angry. I too got angry. At first, It was something that I didn't understand, as we do not need emotions in heaven. It was an extraordinary experience for me. There were times I had to use my powers to escape from the people's hatred towards me, especially their leaders.

They hated me because I testified that the works of the world were evil. They tried to kill me in Judea and stone me in the temple when I told them that I existed before Abraham. I would make myself invisible to avoid being hurt or killed. Even with my great intellect, I found it difficult to comprehend their anger towards me. I was someone who wanted only to love them and to use my powers to get them to love one another, yet I found it a struggle to convince them to do so. There were four long years of hardship, mixed with occasional joy. The raising of Lazarus gave me great joy. I knew that it would convince many of the non-believers. Great multitudes followed me after that as well as when I fed the five thousand. I spoke to the people in parables because that was the only way they could understand. I said to them that the kingdom of heaven was open to those who believed in my Father and me. I also said the two greatest commandments were to love only my Father and to love one another. I knew they would crucify me and give me a horrible death. My Father wanted me to leave, but I begged Him to let me go through with it. He suffered greatly because of my pain. It was my resurrection that was the culmination of everything I had said and done. I appeared to over 500 of my friends and disciples, to get them to believe in me after I'd gone. It pleased both my Father and me when they carried on my work after I had left them. Those are some of the things you should know. The time for speaking in parables or figurative language is now over. These are different times, and they demand different approaches. We have picked your Dr. Clay in the same way that we chose Abraham, Moses, Peter, and all the prophets and disciples. Listen to him, as Dr. Clay will not lead you astray. I will let my words rest with you. When you are ready, I will explain what I need from you, and I ask you to believe what you hear." There was a deep silence before Dr. Clay turned towards the group saying,

"This is the final part of an amazing weekend. All of us need to gather together inside and pool our energies into deciphering what we have heard, and deciding what we should do. I am as flabbergasted as the rest of you. Let us all take a deep breath and gather our thoughts." Dr. Clay was followed by the general into the building, leaving the group in a state of shock, unsure of what to do. Peter was the first to move, followed by Mary-Rose who still looked a little pale. The rest of the group walked silently towards the building until all that was visible was the vapor, which remained quietly suspended against the blue, cloudless, sky.

*   *   *   *

"His voice is so soft, yet commanding," said a dazed-looking Mary-Rose. Everybody sat around the large table in an unorderly fashion as people considered their thoughts.

"He spoke in everyday language like he was one of us," added Lila, to no one in particular. "I had never thought of him as human before. When he was on earth, he must have felt so much torment, both physically and mentally. I feel ashamed that we human beings could have done those things to someone who loved us."

"I don't know where to begin," said John, stirring his coffee cup. "I thought I'd seen everything; now I am confronted with Jesus himself!"

"Is everybody ready to discuss what we've heard?" asked Dr. Clay. Most people shuffled their chairs close to the table. "Okay, let's begin. I want to call on our two theologians, Lila and Peter, to start us off. Could you give us your initial thoughts?" Lila looked towards Peter, who palmed his hand, asking her to go first. Lila pursed her lips as she thought back over Aneesh's words.

"I had asked Peter to reconsider his conversion to believing that Rapoe was God, and unfortunately, things got rather heated. That was before we heard from Aneesh. I hope you have no further surprises for us, Dr. Clay?" Dr. Clay smiled and nodded for her to continue. "Aneesh claims to be Jesus Christ. He certainly spoke as someone with authority; someone who was speaking as an eye witness to events some 2000 years ago. As I mentioned earlier, I feel ashamed if that is the case. How could human beings have such anger and hatred towards someone who only meant them good? From an evidentiary perspective, it is true that many people, especially those in authority, tried to kill him on many occasions. The Gospels say that on more than one occasion that Jesus slipped from view when confronted with their hatred. There is no description of Jesus anywhere in any of the four gospels, which backs up his statement that he had asked St. Peter not to describe him. All in all, I would say that Aneesh comes across as someone who speaks with authority. As to whether or not he's authentic is another matter altogether. I would need to talk with Aneesh in greater detail before offering my judgment." Lila turned to Peter, who said;

"I understand Lila's viewpoint. I found it fascinating listening to how Aneesh describes his home-life. The way he helped Joseph, his earth-father, and how he played with his half-brothers and sisters. He told us that it was his idea to appear as a human being and that his Father agreed with him. Now that we know that God is from another planet far off in the universe, it must have taken many earth years for him to adapt to his body and our ways. That would explain the unwritten gap in his life up to the time he started his ministries. The only other event we know about concerns the preaching in the temple at the age of twelve." Peter paused for a moment before adding, "I'm on the side of the new believers. I'm satisfied that Aneesh is Jesus." The group muttered audibly amongst themselves, while Lila shook her head in dismay.

"Could we have a show of hands of those who believe everything they've witnessed this weekend?" asked Dr. Clay. The noise dissipated as one person looked at another to see if they raised their arms. Dr. Clay raised his arm, accompanied immediately by Mary-Rose and Peter. Zapper finished what he was eating, wiped his hands, and raised his arm high in the air. Then Edgar put his hand up, while Frank put his up reluctantly saying, "I'm doing this purely from a scientific standpoint. Let's say I've moved my flag from the atheist to the agnostic team."

"Count me in too," said a relieved looking Lance. "Once I heard Aneesh, that was it for me." As no other hand showed, Dr. Clay then added,

"So that leaves the 'no' side as Lila, Fred, Laurence, Andrew, and John. Could I call on John to offer his opinion so far? After all, John is the advisor to the world's most significant christian leader." John was hesitant at first, but finally, he relented, saying,

"I don't know what to think, other than I need your help. Andrew has already offered me his support should I decide to recount what I've seen and heard to the powers that be in Rome. I've contemplated lying, but that would be to deny the truth to the people of this world. Thankfully, it is not up to me to decide as to what is right or wrong. That is something that my leaders will have to make. All I can do is report. When they ask me my opinion, I will tell them that I have no reason to doubt what I've witnessed." John sat upright saying, "Off the record. I do believe everything since I heard the voice of Aneesh. That said, I will need the help of those who will go public on the matter. I cannot, and will not, face it alone." John sipped some water as everybody sat in silence." It was Dr. Clay who said,

"I don't think you have any cause to worry on that matter, John. We will all support you every step of the way. Fred, what about you? What are your thoughts?" Fred shuffled uncomfortably in his chair, before saying,

"This weekend was an incredible ride, but I cannot convince myself that there is a creator; someone who made, and continues to make our universe. We are learning more and more every year about our extraordinary universe, and the science continues to lead us away from a divine being to beliefs entirely reliant on physics. If Rapoe, Aneesh, and Mahh, are all genuine figures, then I wholeheartedly welcome the news that they didn't create our planet or us and that they have a home somewhere in a distant part of our universe. I would like to hear about the science that makes up our existence, specifically dark energy. If we knew it's origins, then I can go a long way to considering that these people are the genuine article."

"Well then, let Aneesh answer those questions," interrupted Dr. Clay. The group was taken aback by his statement.

"Is Aneesh still here?" asked Zapper.

"Yes, he's always listening. There's no need for us to go outside. Aneesh has been listening to every word we've said," added Dr. Clay. There was a momentary pause before they heard,

"It's interesting to hear your views. I am encouraged that many of you have seen the light, and I am not surprised that the scientists amongst you still have doubts. Before you ask me specific questions, I must remind you that Mahh has already explained that he too asked these questions but was told that he wouldn't have the capacity to understand the answers until he became his soul. The same applies to each one of you. For me to try to explain to you, today, about the workings of the universe, is akin to me trying to explain to the people 2000 years ago that I am the son of God! Most of those didn't believe. My Father knows the answer to everything, including the origins of your dark energy." Dr. Clay raised his eyebrows, knowing that the scientific world would erupt if they knew that answer.

"Are you saying that Rapoe can explain the origins of dark energy?" asked an incredulous Fred Pinkton. Before Aneesh had time to answer, Mary-Rose stood up and asked,

"Is there a hell?

Epilogue.

"Noel, darling, wake up! Noel, please wake up!" Dr. Clay opened his eyes slowly and saw nothing. Everything was a blur. "Here, take some water," said a familiar voice. Gradually, the blurriness started to clear, and he could make out a figure in front of him.

"Sam - Sammy. Oh my God, what happened?" he said, pushing himself up in the bed. He could see his wife Sam looking at him, holding a glass of water.

"You were stupid, that's what happened. I warned you, but no, Dr. Clay knows everything - as usual," she said in a slightly annoyed tone, but relieved that her husband was back in the land of the living. He took a sip of water and continued to blink, adjusting to the brightness. He looked around and saw that he was in familiar surroundings. Sam sat on the side of the bed, half-smiling and concerned.

"How are you feeling?" she asked. Dr. Clay swallowed and rubbed his face saying,

"What happened? I don't remember a thing," he said worriedly. She looked at him, saying -

"Don't you remember anything about last night? You had nightmares throughout the night. You were shouting in your sleep, and sweating profusely. I can tell you, Dr. Husband, if you ever do anything so stupid again, I might not be around to look after you. Who knows what could have happened? You might have died! Lucky for you I'm a cardiologist, and I could determine that your heart could take it, but as for your mind? Well, that was up to you!" she said, happy now that her husband looked like he was recovering and was compos mentis.

"I don't know what you mean, Sam! Tell me everything." She looked at him alarmed, saying,

"Wow, you are serious! Do you remember we had people over for dinner last night?" Dr. Clay shook his head, remembering nothing. Sam took a deep sigh. "Okay, your best friend, Edgar, his wife Mary-Rose, our neighbor Peter - you do know these people, right?" she said, stopping mid-sentence. Noel's mind rushed through the people's names comparing them with those of his apparent dream. He nodded his confirmation and Sam continued, "We were all enjoying a lovely dinner when Edgar produced his latest drug saying that these were the greatest thing since sliced bread and that we should all try one. There was an argument, and I warned everybody not to take them. Of course, Mary-Rose had a huge argument with Edgar, as usual, but put her eyes to heaven knowing she might as well have been talking to the wall. Peter and Lila had nothing to do with it, while some famous astrophysicist had already popped one into his mouth, contradicting everything that's ever said about one of the world's greatest minds," she said, pausing and looking at him with playful annoyance. "Then we all sat down to watch the new Lance Wilde movie…" Sam stopped when she saw Noel's eyes open wide. His thoughts were all over the place. The images of everything that happened to him came rushing back. He saw Lance Wilde and all of the others on the island. He remembered everything about the weekend just gone. He thought of Rapoe, Aneesh, and Mahh. Then the images of the planet Janza came into view as he stared at Sam. "Are you all right, darling? Do you want me to stop? Can I get you some coffee?" asked Sam, getting worried again. Dr. Clay shook his head and blinked several times, saying,

"No, I'm fine. I'm beginning to remember. Please tell me everything. It's important." Sam licked her lips and stared at him with her doctor's stare and assessed that he was coming back to normal.

"I warned you about taking any hallucinatory drugs. You should know better," Sam scowled. "And I'm never inviting Edgar over to our house again. Do you hear me?" Dr. Clay nodded, silently begging her to continue. "Poor Mary-Rose, that woman deserves more than a medal having to put up with a husband like him." Sam shook her thought away and continued, "As I was saying, we all sat down to watch the new Lance Wilde movie, you know the latest sci-fi that the whole world is talking about called, *'The world of Rapoe,'* with Zapper Zee…" she stopped when she saw Noel look again at her with alarm. She had known many patients who had overdosed on drugs and had treated a number of them. She realized that she had better start treating her husband as if he was her patient.

"Okay, I'll slow down and explain it better. Zapper Zee is one of the best-known musicians on the planet. Mind you; he couldn't act his way out of a paper bag; however, he was starring alongside Wilde, Andrew Johnston, Dan Rosenberg and I can't think of the other guy's name - oh yes, Fred Pinkton. So, they and about fifteen others were the only people left on earth and needed to escape to another planet. They were all on this island somewhere in the Pacific, and seeing they were the last people on the planet, John Mahoney - the character played by Lance - had charted a course to some water planet somewhere in the universe…oh, and this was where my husband fell asleep, and we barely managed to get you upstairs to your bed. Thankfully, Peter was able to help me. Peter was so worried about you. He is a good friend, unlike that, Edgar. Ooooh!" she said, getting angry.

"So, you're saying I didn't see any of this movie?" he asked.

"Nada, my husband, I'm afraid that you were lost in your world. Anyway, the movie was stupid. Some bad guy named Khalid ruled this water planet and he, alongside some general, destroyed the new world, and everybody died. We endured it to the end, and Peter came to the rescue again by helping us get Edgar back on his feet. Mary-Rose was so embarrassed and kept apologizing for Edgar. I was just so relieved to get him the hell out of our house. Never again, Noel, I swear!" Sam stood up and went to the adjoining bathroom. She started to brush her teeth. "Darling, take it easy for the rest of the day. It's Sunday, so there's nothing on your schedule. I've already canceled the lunch we were meant to have with the Bardsley's," she announced from the bathroom. Noel remained seated upright in the bed. The swirling thoughts and images continued to rush through his brain. *"Everything was so real,* he thought. *"Lance, Zapper, Khalid, Edgar…everybody. Rapoe, Aneesh, Mahh!"*

Noel looked out the window at the sun rising and saw how beautiful it was. He breathed out a long sigh as everything became clear. *"It was all a dream!"* he thought. *"Yet, it was all so real. There was so much that if any of it…"* "Sam, Sam, was there something in that movie about a light?" he asked aloud so that Sam could hear him. Sam peered back into the room, holding her toothbrush in her hand and a quizzical look on her face.

"How did you know anything about *'the light'*? That didn't materialize until the very end," she said quizzically.

"I remember something about *'a light,'* answered Noel.

"*The light'* was the whole point of the picture. When the good guys reached the water planet, they were guided by this light, which was supposed to represent the beginning of creation or something. I don't know, as we had all lost interest by that stage. It's strange how you know anything about it because you were' light's *out'* long before that scene came into the picture," she said, laughing at her humor, as she returned to brushing her teeth. Dr. Clay looked back out through the window and saw a small cumulus cloud with what appeared like a piercing light through its center. He put his hands to his temples as he heard his voice saying to him -

"My name is…"

The End.

Other books by the same author;

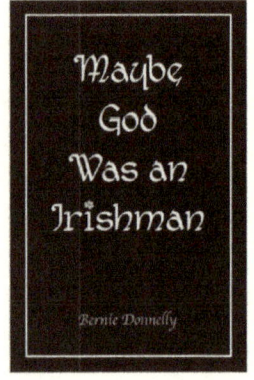

The novel centers on the real-world wonders that certain people are able to achieve through kindness, compassion, patience and self-sacrifice. Perhaps there is such a thing as divine intervention and the gentle nudging of God, but the tangible miracles of good-hearted humans are often even more powerful. The end of this novel will leave readers uplifted and refreshed – spiritually, emotionally and philosophically – regardless of one's particular religious' beliefs or opinions. That is the sign of a truly great book, and a very talented writer." SPR Review - 2017

"Maybe God Is an American" reveals what happens after Father Sean disappears, and welcomes readers into a new adventure on the other side of the pond. The simplicity and beauty of which Donnelly expresses universal truths, and presents moral imperatives, is truly impressive. He has hit on an unforgettable premise in these first two books, and created something that readers of any creed or country can appreciate."
SPR Review - 2017

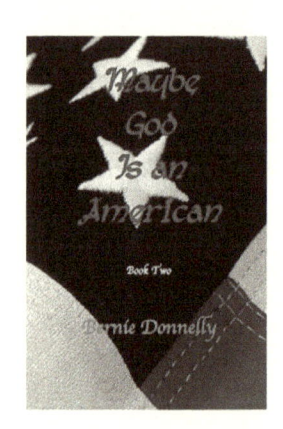

Frank McGovern has not lived a traditionally "good" life, being disloyal to his wife and a distant father to his son. However, when an accident befalls him and his existence is transformed overnight, something rather miraculous happens. In the struggle to find his way back into the land of the living, he must also traverse the long road that brought him to this point. These realizations come back in fits and starts, worked in expertly by the author, so readers are essentially rebuilding the puzzle of McGovern's life right along with him. SPR review June'1

In 3 days, events throughout the world are dictating catastrophes, yet the scientists refuse to believe what their instruments are telling them. Super-psychic, Gladys Lawson, has also seen the signs, and wonders how she can convince the world that something cataclysmic is about to occur? Time is running out for Gladys, the scientists, and the rest of humanity!

DEAR DAUGHTER

Bernie Donnelly

This debut work of "creative nonfiction" relates an Irish entrepreneur's tumultuous professional and personal life. The son of a film projectionist and a factory worker, he fights his way to the upper echelons of the software industry and ultimately becomes a multimillionaire. His strategies are gutsy, and his distinctive personality is his greatest asset: he's forceful, driven, occasionally oblivious, and very funny. In addition to his business triumphs and defeats, he goes through two marriages, the births of multiple children, a battle with cancer, and the loss of his father. His tale is also loaded with humorous tales that cover everything from a bacchanalian trip to South Africa to his own man-hating dog. Throughout all of these accounts he shines as an eminently charming narrator

Bruce and Keiko are two people who would never have imagined that their lives would cross. Bruce has become resigned to living a life alone while Keiko had experienced trauma that was not of her making. Both would end up helping one another through their anguish; revealing their true pasts and making them understand that there's always hope as long as you try to find it. Heartfelt and memorable, Keiko is an exceptional novel about finding love late in life.

KEIKO
By Bernie Donnelly

All original stories and poems that should delight any 7 to 10 year-old. It was written in a style that should make the reader happy too.

Preview of the new book "Leo the Liar" due out 2020.

Leo

"I'll have another pint and the same for my friend," said the fat man to the bartender.

Dublin airport was as busy as ever with the aimless faces moving hither and thither, walking and rushing, lost, excited, confused, focused, and frustrated. The tempers flared alongside the laughter of arriving stag and hen parties, making their way to continue to blot out their mundane lives in a city that welcomed their antics and their euros. Others cried at the parting gates knowing that their love for their loved ones had to be non-physical for either a short time or forever.

These were the things the fat man pondered and noticed as the barman did his magic pouring pints of Guinness with shamrock crests sitting atop their creamy beds; while gins, whiskeys, and brandies lined up in parallel with the rows of pint glasses of lagers that were being distributed to welcome the thirsty souls who needed the courage and the stimulus that only alcohol could provide.

"Ah, there you are," said the lanky looking man with braided hair climbing up on to the barstool. "I hope you didn't order me another pint, did you?" he asked, speaking in a deep, rich tone, which didn't match his torn-denim appearance or skinny look. He drank a quarter of his pint while waiting for an answer.

"Enjoy it, Leo. You have a long journey ahead of you," responded the fat man.

"So, listen, George. Let me give you my phone number, and we'll stay in touch when I get back from the States," added Leo. The fat man, now known as George, took out his phone and started to key in some details.

"What's your number?" he asked. Leo called out his numbers in his melodic voice which made people take notice of the gorgeous Irish accent emanating from the strangely handsome young man with the pronounced green eyes. George looked up at the airport monitor saying, "Isn't that your flight to Orlando closing at gate 24?" Leo took another gulp of his drink while he studied the screen.

"It'll be fine. I've loads of time," responded Leo, while George shrugged relishing the arrival of his new pint of Guinness.

"I keep thinking I've seen you before somewhere. You look very familiar," said George. Leo looked confidently back at him saying,

"Afraid not, George. No fame as yet, but I'm working on it," he smiled, taking another drink.

"So you're the head engineer on some new bridge in Miami?" asked George, impressed by his new-found friend.

"It'll be the largest structure in Florida by the time it's finished," responded Leo with the confidence of a man in control of his destiny. "I have over 500 men working under me, and I'll be glad when it's finished. I landed this particular job due to my work on London's 'Rolling Bridge.' Have you ever heard of it?" George shook his head and wiped the cream off his lips.

"Can't say I have."

"It was designed by my great friend, Thomas - or Tommy as I call him - Heatherwick, who was commissioned to design a bridge that allowed pedestrians to cross an inlet of the Grand Union Canal at Paddington Basin while also allowing the admittance to the boat that resides there. A very tricky problem, but myself and Tommy figured it all out to everyone's satisfaction. Got great kudos on that one," continued Leo finishing off the rest of his pint.

George looked at Leo with admiration in his eyes and wondered at his unorthodox use of the English language. "That's some achievement for someone so young. How old did you say you were again?" he asked with growing curiosity.

"Twenty-eight."

"Give me the name of the bridge in Miami, so I can Google it and tell everybody I met the man that built it," added George enthusiastically.

"I'd better make a move because I don't think they'll wait for me," responded Leo hurriedly, jumping down from his seat and gathering his things, while managing to ignore George's request.

"You say you're traveling first class," asked George, while Leo scrambled for his tatty looking hold-all which matched his demeanor.

"Business-class, George. I don't think they have first-class any more. I'll be sure to get in touch upon my return," he added while flinging the hold-all over his shoulder and waving goodbye at the same time, as he headed towards his gate. George waved him off, still smiling with admiration for a young man who will go far in life. His admiration turned to one of disappointment some twenty minutes later when George realized that Leo had stuck him with the check!

"Would Mr. Leo Butler, please go to gate 24," announced a cross-sounding woman over the tannoy system. "This is a final boarding call as the gate is now closing," she said aloud. Leo quickened his pace.

   *   *   *   *

"Can I get you some refreshment, Mrs. Waters?" asked the flight attendant to the kindly looking lady seated at the business class window.

"No, thank you, it's a little too early for me to imbibe," responded the lady.

"Perhaps a soft drink, or maybe some iced water?" enthused the stewardess.

"Well then, perhaps a little water," she replied.

"Certainly. By the way, my name's Rose, and if there's anything I can do to make your trip more enjoyable, then please let me know. We should be taking off shortly. We're just waiting on one more passenger to arrive," she informed Mrs. Waters and the other business-class passengers in ear-shot who were browsing their menus and looking forward to seeing the latest movie offerings.

"How's it going there, missus," said Leo in a scratchy Dublin voice, bearing no resemblance to the accent he had left at the bar. He pushed his carry-on into the locker above his seat. "Looks like we'll be manacled together for the duration of the journey - what?" said Leo, not bothered in the slightest by the annoyed stares in his direction knowing that Leo happened to be the one that delayed the entire plane. Mrs. Waters looked aghast at the audaciously loud young man with his braided hair and a slight ponytail, who looked like he needed a good wash. She was still speechless as he settled himself into his seat beside her, kicking off his sneakers and stretching his legs out far, trying to get as comfortable as possible.

"Please fasten your seatbelt, sir, and don't extend your seat or your footrest until we are fully airborne," said flight attendant Rose, thinking that this passenger looked like trouble from the get-go.

"Oh miss, I think I will have that drink now if you don't mind," said the old lady pleadingly.

"Certainly, Mrs. Waters. What can I get you?"

"A gin and tonic - on ice, please." She took another look at her unwanted companion and turned back towards the stewardess, saying - "Oh, and make it a double." The stewardess nodded affirmatively with understanding in her voice.

"Eh, I wouldn't mind a cold beer if you're buying," interrupted Leo, looking at the stewardess's nametag and adding with a smiling face - 'Rose' is it?" The stewardess looked at him with disgust, trying to smile and do her job.

"I'll bring you a Heineken," she added, turning towards the galley.

"Jaysus, this is great, what?" added Leo, smiling at his new companion. "Free drinks all the way and some good grub too. This is the life - what?" he repeated. Leo opened the plastic bags containing the headphones, courtesy slippers, and a small blanket. He rifled through the net at the back of the seat in front of him, like some tramp looking for lost treasure.

"Mrs. Waters, I heard Rose call you," added Leo, flicking through the pages of the in-flight magazine. "The name's Leo...Leo Butler. Very pleased to make your acquaintance," he said, holding out his right hand while holding on to his new-found belongings with his left hand. Mrs. Waters stared at his outstretched hand and then at his face. She wondered how such a ruffian could afford to travel business-class, and how she could have been so unfortunate to have her vacation of a lifetime tarnished by his presence? She sighed deeply and offered her hand, saying -

"I'm Mary Waters. I'm pleased to make your acquaintance. The only thing is I have a shocking headache, and I'm afraid I won't be much company. I intend to sleep most of the journey," she said matter-of-factly.

"Not a problem there, Mary. I won't make your headache any worse than it is. Tell me, is this your first time going to the States?" he asked enthusiastically, wanting to engage in as much conversation as there was left in the old lady before she dozed off. Mary Waters took a large mouthful of her newly served gin and tonic and hoped its effects would be quick. She waited for its taste to wash her throat before deciding how to answer this unwanted person in her life.

"It's my first trip to Florida. I have a sister in Washington DC, whom I have visited on several occasions," she concluded taking another large sip of her drink.

"And what do you work at?" inquired Leo, guzzling half the bottle of Heineken in one gulp, and not bothering to use the plastic container that accompanied it. Mary sighed deeply and placed her drink on her side, armrest.

"Ladies and gentlemen, please ensure your tabletops are in the upright position, and your seatbelts are secure," announced the chief steward on the intercom.

"Perhaps we can continue our conversation as soon as we're airborne," suggested Mary, as the plane taxied the runway.

"Fair enough, Mary," added Leo, throwing back the last gulp of his Heineken and flipping the pages of the magazine. Mary Waters turned her head towards her window as the plane lifted off the ground. She peered down over Dublin city as the airplane maneuvered its position to its flight-path. As the aircraft lifted towards the shies, she could identify most of the various landmarks, but she was unable to locate her home town of Killiney. She thought back to the week just gone, and how she had managed to organize her teachers so that everybody knew what it was, they should do while she was away. Mary was the principal at the Holy Child Secondary School for the past thirty years in the very upmarket part of greater Dublin known as Killiney. She was due to retire at the end of the current school term and was proud of her school's achievements. Mary had been responsible for many new creative ideas including the award-winning choir, and of course the "Maeve Binchy Library" - named after their most famous literary past pupil. She smiled with contentment on a career that had avoided any controversies and continued to have its reputation enhanced. Yes, she felt justified in rewarding herself with a business-class trip that -

"So, tell us, Mary, what do you work at?" added the nasal sounding voice that shattered her happy thoughts while the airplane leveled off. Mary sighed again and realized that she would either have to engage her ruffian companion in some meaningful conversation while she thought of an excellent excuse to ignore him.

"I'm a teacher," she said, looking around for the stewardess to replenish her now empty glass.

"Jaysus, that's a coincidence - what? So am I," announced Leo with a beaming smile.

"Oh mother of all that is holy, rescue me from this torment," prayed Mary silently.

"Really!" she managed to say, thankful that the stewardess saw her waving hand and realized her dilemma. The stewardess nodded and assured her silently that remedial action was forthcoming.

"That's amazing - what? What do you teach, Mary?" enthused Leo, happy that he'd hit upon a mutually exciting subject. Mary continued to stare in his direction, unsure what she should say, or how she was going to disentangle herself from this unbelievably annoying toad.

"I'm a principal at *'The Holy Child School in Killiney'*," she said, hoping that maybe her boast might shut him up.

"Jaysus, that's a bit of all right there, Mary. Killiney! It doesn't get any more up-market than that," he said, looking around for someone to replace his empty bottle with a six-pack. Mary looked at the back of his neck and got a good glimpse of his dangling ponytail. She wondered had the Irish education system deteriorated so much that this was what was teaching our youth?

"So tell me. Where and what do you teach?" Mary decided to ask out of abject curiosity.

"This is the captain speaking. We have now reached our altitude height, so you can now unfasten your seatbelts if you wish, although we do recommend keeping them fastened in case of unexpected turbulence. We hope you have an enjoyable flight."

"Eh, Miss. Could I have a few beers over here when you're ready," said Leo in a loud voice aimed at the galley area where all of the flight attendants were busy getting everything ready. Rose turned and looked at him, distastefully. She forced a half-smile that others could immediately interpret as being something you'd manage to do when faced with someone that had just spilled a glass of red wine on your new carpet. Leo was undeterred by her reaction, as he held the bottle on-high and shook it with a wide-eyed smile while putting up four fingers with his other hand indicating that one bottle wouldn't be enough to satisfy his desperate thirst. He turned to Mary,

"Sorry, Mary. What were you saying?"

"I was asking you where and what do you teach?" she repeated, checking her watch. She couldn't believe that only twenty minutes had elapsed since she became burdened with everybody's worst houseguest. She calculated that she still had other eight-plus hours to go, which made her shut her eyes in despair.

"I teach maths out in Darndale, Mary. A bit different to your Killiney - Right?" he offered, happy to see a tray of drinks heading in his direction. Mary was shocked. If she had been asked to guess his occupation; never in a million years would she have suspected he was in the same profession as her. She found the fact inconceivable and tried to rack her brains for a follow-up question that would expose him for what he surely wasn't.

"Mathematics, you say?" she asked and answered.

"Yeh, and a bit of history. I like a little bit of history," added Leo, grabbing one of the four bottles of Heineken placed on his table by Rose, who continued to give him the evil-eye as she placed another large gin and tonic on Mary's tray.

"Specifically, what level of mathematics do you teach?" asked Mary.

"Final year - honors maths," answered Leo with an assuredness that made Mary raise her eyebrows with more than a little surprise.

"Mathematics and history are two of my favorite subjects," offered Mary, happy to stay on this line of questioning so that she could expose this fraud. She was rising to the challenge of squashing this insect so that she could at least enjoy the majority of her luxury flight.

Mary could more than match any scholar in any debate on European history, especially if it concerned the nineteenth and twentieth centuries. She also knew that any school in Darndale couldn't possibly have anything remotely like an honors subject in mathematics. The final year certificate in honors mathematics was as tricky a subject as it was for any mid-term graduate student. She had never been to Darndale, but she knew that it was situated somewhere in the northern part of Dublin. She also knew that it was a deprived area with many social problems, and was not the place to go for any self-respecting individual at any time of the day or night. She sipped her drink and relaxed as she said,

"I didn't realize that your school had an honors mathematics curriculum?"

Leo opened up the second of his four screw-cap bottles and gulped down practically three-quarters in one go. He wiped his lips saying -

"Aaah, that's a lot better. It's funny how beer gets better, the more you drink - Wha'" he suggested. "Yeh, there's a good few…students, as you call them that sat the recent exam. Although they wouldn't take too kindly to anyone calling them students. More like - 'the lads,' - you know what I'm saying there, Mary?" Mary decided to ignore his Dublinese phraseology and move quickly to the task of exposing him.

"What mathematics subjects - specifically - do you teach?" Leo leaned forward in his seat and tried to scratch his back, but it was out of reach of his fingers.

"Would you mind scratching me back there, Mary. I have a terrible itch, and I can't reach it?"

"Certainly not," she said abruptly. Leo immediately stood up and leaned his back against the edge of his seat, rubbing the itching part while ooh-ing and ahh-ing at the same time.

"Jaysus, that's a lot better. I sometimes get these crazy itches that drive me mental. "He sat back down again; drained the last of his beer, and continued talking.

"The usual stuff, Mary. Sequences and series, although algebra and calculus also play a big part," he said confidently. "Some of the sequences and series questions can be pretty challenging but can expose a lively debate - you know, like? For example, in the recent Leaving cert questions, some of my guys were disappointed with the questions, as they didn't challenge them enough. One of the lads told me that question one was easy-peasy, while questions three and four were very doable once the lads realized that calculus was what was required. They were trick questions, but my lads saw right through them. The lads were 'delirah' that Proof of De Moivre's theorem appeared. When I saw the paper, I thought that Section B was fair enough, as it returned to the topic of exponential functions with the usual mix of algebra, graphs, and calculus. I have to say that I was pretty pleased with the ol' results though. I think we came in first in the greater Dublin area - North side of the city, that is, Mary." Leo opened another bottle of Heineken and slurped contentedly while staring at the television screen in front of him, which was showing some insipid type of cartoon. If he had looked at his traveling companion, he would have seen a person more than a little bemused.

 Mary was amazed. She continued to stare at the newly promoted - ruffian to *'man-of-mystery'* - who continued to gaze at his TV screen and guffaw out loud at something that was tickling his sense of humor. Mary was more than a little bemused at how this person had spoken effortlessly, and with some authority, on what was regarded as one of the most difficult final year mathematics papers in recent times. She wondered this person claims that his students, not only sat the examination but skipped through the questions with ease, achieving results that other - more reputable schools - had tried and failed to deliver! She decided to go on the offensive.

"I believe you have a point. I do know that my students found the mathematics papers particularly difficult this time around. Tell me, what about your views on the honors history papers?" asked Mary of Leo who was laughing aloud at the antics of the cartoon characters on his screen.

"Jaysus, Mary - this *Incredibles'* movie is great. I think it's even better than the first one. Did you see it?" Mary took another large sip of her drink, trying desperately to temper her mood, while at the same time trying to make sense of this contradiction of a human being.

"Eh...no. I haven't. I was asking you your opinion on the honors history papers. Did your stud...lads, find that easy too?" she asked, not having the slightest idea what answer she was going to receive.

"History! Ah yeh, that was a toughie all right, Mary. Let me think. Yeh, the lads thought it was a load of bollocks. They said that too many case-study questions, especially those concerning the options on the Nation States and international tensions and dictatorship and democracy. The period covering 1912-1949, also had two very straight forward questions on the Eucharistic Congress and Ireland during World War 2. Another on Anglo-Irish relations was nice, as it had appeared in previous papers. I liked the question on the civil rights movement, but the Apprentice Boys one was a bit tricky. There was a straightforward question on Martin Luther King and the Montgomery Bus Boycott, and a generous question that asked students to discuss two presidents, from Roosevelt to Reagan," continued Leo, leaning forward to uncap another Heineken. Mary couldn't have been more shocked or impressed. Leo was more than a contradiction; he was a philosophical quandary. Anyone who dared to offer an assessment based on his appearance would have been wrong before they opened their mouth. If having spent time in his company - without the proper examination - someone would have come away without granting him the time of day and happy to be rid of him. Mary, not only had a considered opinion of her new companion - but one that was enamored to the point of view of profound respect. She took another sip of her drink, making a mental note not to order anymore, as she had far exceeded her limit of alcohol intake. It also reminded her that she needed to visit the ladies room before she had an accident.

"Would you excuse me, Leo. I need to visit the bathroom," she said, standing up and waiting for Leo to untangle himself.

"Goin' for a lcak, Mary - Wha'?" he said aloud, moving his legs in an angular manner, allowing Mary to shuffle into the aisle. Mary hoped and prayed that nobody assumed that they were related.

"When you gotta go, you gotta go," said Leo aloud to nobody in particular, bringing stares of criticism from some people, while others shook their heads in dismay, or tried to ignore him altogether. The stewardess had been looking in Leo's direction the whole time, and she decided that she'd had enough. She smiled at the passengers as she made her way to Leo's seat. She bent down and said firmly but quietly,

"Sir, I have to insist that you remain quiet, as you are disturbing the other passengers. Is that understood?" she said, as Leo smiled back at her saying,

"Not a problem there, Rose. Mum's the word," he said, putting his finger to his lips making a shushing sound. "Could I trouble you for another Heineken?" The stewardess couldn't believe his audacity.

"Not for the moment. I think you've had enough to drink for the time being. Besides, we're all out of Heineken as you've drunk the lot." Leo smiled back in a non-confrontational manner, saying -

"Not a problem. Whatever you have in the beer stakes will do nicely. Whenever you're ready - like." She looked at him exasperatedly saying,

"We're about to serve dinner. Afterward, I'll see what I have to offer by way of beer, but please behave yourself." With that, she turned back towards the galley while Leo put his headphones on and continued to watch the movie.

Mary studied herself in the bathroom mirror, and she knew for sure that she'd over imbibed. "I'd better put a stop to this drinking," she murmured, as she touched up her lips with lipstick and brushed her hair. She straightened her skirt and jacket saying - "Right. Back to the battlefront."

She made her way back to her seat and wobbled slightly grabbing on to the headrests as she tried to steady herself. She smiled embarrassingly and clambered back into her seat. She had begun to feel an on-coming warmth towards Leo until she heard him say -

"Grubs on the way, Mary. Rose took the orders while you were away. I took the liberty of ordering you a salad for starters, is that alright?" Mary gave a deep sigh as she heard him speak in his gravely Dublin accent.

"Yes, a salad is fine," she replied. She then considered Leo's words and was surprised at his thoughtfulness.

"I thought you looked like a salad person. Meself, I prefer the old soup, and I couldn't resist ordering the chicken curry for the main meal. I saw they had some fish on the menu, but I wasn't sure you wanted fish or the steak," he said, looking around him like a thirteen-year-old. Mary blinked and raised her eyes in further surprise, saying -

"Thank you, but I will go for the fish when the stewardess returns. She took out her tray from the armrest and set it with the plastic cutlery wrapped within the cloth napkin.

"Do you fancy sharing a bottle of vino with the dinner, Mary?" asked Leo, as if he was talking to his best friend. Mary could see that Leo was not going to let her alone, and she decided she might as well shoulder on as best she could, hoping that perhaps either one of them might collapse with exhaustion or, in Leo's case, alcohol fatigue.

"Why not," she responded much to Leo's delight.

"Great stuff," he said aloud. "Eh, Rose - whenever you're ready," he announced boldly to the stewardess who was busily organizing the other passengers with their meals. She ignored Leo and turned towards the people opposite, asking them if they'd like red or white wine with their meals.

"A bottle of your finest red, Rose - whenever you can," he said aloud across the aisles, without a care in the world and not bothered in the slightest that he was interrupting her with the other passengers. Rose breathed out deeply, knowing full-well that her efforts at controlling her unruly passenger were like trying to swim against the current. She moved over towards them, and before she could say anything, Mary interjected, saying -

"I'm afraid it's all my fault, Rose. I had suggested to Leo that we should share a bottle of wine." Rose turned her face of disgust from Leo and changed her expression to one of caring, as she smiled in Mary's direction.

"Not a problem, Mrs. Waters. I have a cabernet or a Pinot Noir."

"Cab-or-Net, as we say over in Darndale," said Leo, making himself more comfortable and relishing the forthcoming imbibement. Rose ignored him by pouring out one glass of Cabernet for Mary and leaving the bottle on Leo's tray beside his empty glass while struggling to hide her annoyance at the same time.

"Thanks-a-mill, Rose," said Leo, filling up his glass to the brim.

"I wonder, could I bother you for the fish?" asked Mary.

"Certainly, Mrs. Waters. "added Rose, squinting her eyes in disgust in Leo's direction, who was utterly unmoved by her expression.

"Cheers, Mary," said Leo, as he waited to clink glasses.

"Slainte," responded Mary as both glasses clinked noisily due to Leo's exuberance in nearly knocking Mary's drink out of her hand.

"A bit of the ole' Gaeilge there, Mary. I have to say I was never one for speaking Irish. Could never get the hang of it," he said wistfully, stretching himself further in his seat and holding his glass of wine lovingly in both hands. Mary had decided to throw in the towel and not bother to interrogate Leo any further. She believed he could hold his own in any conversation about any part of the school syllabus. She took another sip of her wine and sat upright to enjoy her meal which Rose now placed before her. Leo grabbed his spoon and proceeded to demolish his soup bowl in less than a minute, while Mary had barely managed to fork her salad.

"My, you must be famished," she said, as Leo wiped his mouth with his napkin saying -

"Jaysus, that was bleedin' great. I could eat bowls of that stuff. Can't wait for the curry," he added, taking a large gulp of the wine. Mary needed to know something. She pondered her question and then realized that anything she would ask of Leo would have no bearing whatsoever on his feelings - one way or the other.

"Tell me, Leo. How come you managed to travel business-class on a teacher's salary?" Leo stared in the direction of the galley, hoping that his curry was on the way.

"That's me, Da for you. Yeh, Da paid for the lot. He's a great man. You know, he has his plane. Yep, that's right - a fully qualified pilot. He's able to get cheap upgrades, so he had no problem getting me the ticket." Mary creased her forehead and pursed her lips, reasoning that what Leo had said made perfect sense.

"He's a pilot, you say? Is that his full-time occupation?"

"No. That's just a hobby. He used to fly with Delta, but he gave that up years ago. He's a writer. I think he got nominated for the Booker prize one year," added Leo, finishing off the rest of his wine while replenishing both of their glasses.

"The Booker Prize!" exclaimed Mary with great admiration upon learning this news. "Why that's astonishing. Do you realize how difficult it is to be nominated? Tell me, what books has he written?"

"Aw great. Here's me curry," said Leo, ignoring Mary's enthusiasm as he rubbed his hands in expectation of the food.

"What's your father's name?" she pushed, dying to know if this was the reason behind Leo's intelligence?

"Give me a minute there, Mary. First things first. You know what I'm sayin'?" he said, rubbing his hands gleefully as the piping hot curry in front of him. Mary watched him and couldn't help but smile, watching him enjoying his meal. She drank some more wine as she watched him eat and became more mystified at a man who displayed a total disregard for any usual civilities while at the same time he stored a wealth of knowledge and academic brilliance that contradicted his civic bereftness. As she was about to pursue her questions about his talented father, the plane shook suddenly, and some people made frightened noises. Mary grabbed Leo's arm and tensed. The aircraft continued to shudder, and the flight attendants moved quickly to their seats and buckled themselves. Rose grabbed the intercom phone and announced,

"Ladies and gentlemen, please return to your seats and fasten your seatbelts. We are experiencing some unexpected turbulence." Mary continued to hold Leo's arm tightly as she gazed towards Rose and then at the other attendants looking for solace, but found that they seemed decidedly anxious. She turned towards Leo, who had a beaming smile on his face. He patted Mary's hand saying,

"Take another slurp of the vino there, Mary. You'll be alright. Leo's here to protect you." Mary took his advice and finished off the rest of her wine.

"Where's the bottle of wine?" she asked, not seeing it on the table.

"Not to worry there, Mary. Leo always gets his priorities right. I made sure it was the first thing to be saved in the crisis," he said, topping up Mary's glass.

"This is the captain speaking. I'm sorry about the sudden turbulence, but we should be clear of it in a moment or so. I'm climbing a little higher which should get us out of it. Please remain seated with your seatbelts securely fastened."

"There you go, Mary. Nothing to worry about." Mary had her eyes shut tightly and began to pray.

"In times of crisis, we should always make sure to call on all the help we can. I think it was the French philosopher, Sartre, who on his deathbed declared that he wanted to convert to Catholicism. As the priest performed the baptismal rites, he asked Sartre did he reject Satan. Sartre responded that he didn't think it was the appropriate time to be making enemies," continued Leo, but Mary wasn't listening. She continued to drink her wine in large gulps until the plane eventually settled into its regular steady pattern.

"You're all right now, Mary?" assured Leo. Mary no longer had her eyes shut tight. Instead, she looked like she had fallen asleep. Leo pushed her gently, saying, "Mary. Mary. Are you all right? Are you asleep?" There was no response, and then Leo heard her gentle snores. He pressed the button that made her seat fully recline and took her glass and covered her with his blanket, closing the shutter on her window and turned out her light. He smiled as he patted the back of her hand. "Nothing to worry about, my dear. Your favorite traveling companion will make sure you sleep soundly," he said reverting to his airport bar persona and abandoning his Dublin accent. He settled into his seat and put on his headphones and tuned to the jazz music channel not having noticed that Rose had been peeping through the curtains at him from the galley mystified at this puzzle of a human being.

*   *   *   *

"Ladies and gentlemen, welcome to Orlando International airport. Please make sure you collect all of your belongings before alighting from the aircraft. We enjoyed looking after you and hope to see you all again soon. Slan agus beannacht," said the flight attendant.

Leo unbuckled his seatbelt and gathered his things. He looked at Mary Waters and saw that she was still in a deep sleep. He smiled at how comfortable she looked and turned towards the galley, looking for Rose. He was mildly startled to see her standing beside him.

"What's wrong with Mrs. Waters?" she asked, looking concerned.

"I'd say she had one or two too much. Wouldn't imagine the ol' bod is able for the drinkies. You know what I'm sayin' there, Rose?" Rose gently nudged Mrs. Waters, who mumbled incoherently.

"This is all your fault. I saw you plying Mrs. Waters with alcohol the entire trip," added an annoyed Rose.

"Maybe you should order a wheelie chair for her," responded Leo, ignoring Rose's pointed accusation. "It was a lovely flight, Rose. I enjoyed it. Tell Mrs. Waters she's one of the best." He then offered Rose a handshake which surprised her, even more, when she accepted it, watching Leo alight the plane without a care in the world. It was after he left that she looked at her hand and found a €100 note folded neatly in her palm.

"Goodness gracious," she exclaimed and looked around her, wondering if anybody had noticed. "I've never had anybody give me a tip before," she muttered quietly, looking back down at her hand and the generous note looking back up at her. Mrs. Waters started to murmur herself awake. Rose took her blanket, saying - "Remain seated, Mrs. Waters. I'll get you some water to drink. There's no rush. I'll have somebody here to help you in a few minutes." Rose couldn't believe what had just happened. *"Of all the people..."* she thought, but then one of the crew needed her attention, and her thoughts went back to her work.

Author Profile

Bernie Donnelly was born in Dublin in 1953. He formed his own technology company in his early twenties and built up business operations in Ireland, England, and India.

He has an avid interest in history and astronomy. He has five children and one step-daughter. He lives with his wife, Keiko, in Sarasota, Florida.